# PLAGUES AND FEDERATION

Scholastic Press
345 Pacific Highway
Lindfield NSW 2070
an imprint of Scholastic Australia Pty Ltd (ACN 000 614 577)
PO Box 579
Gosford NSW 2250
www.scholastic.com.au

Part of the Scholastic Group
Sydney ● Auckland ● New York ● Toronto ● London ● Mexico City
● New Delhi ● Hong Kong

First published in 2000
Text copyright © Vashti Farrer, 2000.

National Library of Australia Cataloguing-in-Publication entry
    Farrer, Vashti.
    Plagues and Federation: the diary of Kitty Barnes, the Rocks, 1900.
    ISBN 1 86504 266 8.
    1. Plagues – Australia – Juvenile fiction.
    2. Australia – History – 1891-1901 – Juvenile fiction.
    I. Title. (Series: My story).
A823.3

Cover design by Antart, Sydney

Typeset in Times New Roman.

Printed by McPherson's Printing Group, Maryborough Vic.

10 9 8 7 6 5 4 3 2 1             0 1 2 3 4 5 / 0

MY STORY

# PLAGUES AND FEDERATION

The Diary of Kitty Barnes,
The Rocks, Sydney, 1901

## by Vashti Farrer

A Scholastic Press book
from
Scholastic Australia

*This diary belongs to*

*Kitty Barnes*
*88 Windmill Street*
*The Rocks*
*Sydney*
*Australia*
*The World*
*The Universe.*

*If found please return.*
*Reward.*

Dear Diary,

My name is Kitty Barnes. My teacher Miss Collins says I'm to write something every day, only not if it's just to say it's sunny or raining like. First but, I'm going to write about my family.

There's nine of us kids, four at home still.

Bertie my favourite brother's 22 and been humping his bluey up country since he were 16. He's learnt to ride a horse and all, only now he's come back to Sydney to enlist to fight the Boojers (that's what he calls the Boers) in South Africa. The army give him leave from his barracks last night, on account of it was New Year's Eve and why shouldn't he have a good time I say, if he's off to fight a war?

After Bertie comes George. He's 21 and works in a funeral parlour. He lives over the shop only I don't know how he can. It gives me the creeps.

Then there's Ethel, 18, packs boots in a factory, and Dolly, 16, and in pickles. They share a room in a boarding house over Chippendale way, so's to be near their factories.

Next comes Mabel, she's 15 and in service and lives in with a family at Darlinghurst. She has her own attic room and all.

I'm after her and Ma thinks I'm a right handful. She says it's because I got red hair, like hers, only I think it's because I don't always do what she says.

After me there's Fred, 11, and Artie, 9, then Clara May, Maisie for short. She's 6 and the baby and her two front teeth is missing.

Even though it were New Year's Eve Sunday, everything was shut, just like any other Sunday. When night time come but, the streets were chockablock with people out singing and shouting and all enjoying theirselves. The churches stayed open but, till after midnight to see the old year out. Us younger kids weren't allowed to stay up real late, only Bertie was out all night just about. I know, cos I heard him come creeping in real early yesterday morning hoping Ma wouldn't hear him.

Our house is the browny yellow one with its paint peeling near the corner of Ferry Lane. It's a one up, one downer. Ma and Pa got the bed in the room upstairs. Me, Fred, Artie and Maisie got to share two mattresses on the floor. It's a bit cramped so if any of the others come home of a night unexpected, they got to doss downstairs.

There's lots of houses round our way. All sort of squashed in and climbing up the hillsides, higgledy-piggledy like. Ma says it look like a rabbit warren only it's not too bad, just some of the streets are real narrow and the drains don't work proper and the privies smell.

Pa used to be a rag and bone man for all the houses round here, only he lost his horse and cart in the depression when the banks crashed. Now he does labouring jobs of a day when he can get them, which is not all that often, so Ma has to take in washing and ironing to help make ends meet.

We used to go to Millers Point School only Pa can't afford it no more so now we go to Ragged School down in Harrington Street. It's for orphans mainly and poor kids whose pas got no work so it don't cost nothing, only you're s'posed to leave soon as you turn 13.

Miss Collins give me this diary when I tell her I want to be a lady typist in a big office with a typewriter all my own. Or maybe one of them switchboard ladies as plugs in wires for the telephones. I'd like that and I can talk real posh too. 'Just connecting!' I'd say or, 'Sorry he can't talk right now. He's real busy'. Sometimes I pretend I'm a switchboard lady with the handles of my skipping rope that I got for Christmas, only when no one's looking.

Ma won't agree, but. She says I'm to leave school and go into service, same as she did and Mabel, to help out, but it's all right for Mabel, she wants to be a lady's maid. I DON'T.

Miss Collins says 1900'll be a good year for a diary, seeing as how it's the last year of the 19th century. This time next year, we might have a federation. That's one big country, not six separate colonies like now. She says Australia's a bit like an old lady now with lots of parcels to carry and she keeps dropping them so it'd be much better if she tied them all up together like.

I've put 'please return' on the first page, because I don't want no one reading it. I'm not sure about the reward bit. I've only got my skipping rope and it might be a boy like Reggie Cook from next door, as finds it and what would he do with a skipping rope?

After tea, of a night, Pa reads to us from the newspaper.
The *Sydney Morning Herald* costs a whole penny to buy
but Pa gets it for nothing out of a bin near the tram stop
where this gent drops them when he's finished.
Sometimes they're a day old but that don't matter to Pa.
He still brings them home.

Last night he read this bit out about plague.

I said, 'What plague?'

He said, 'The bubonic.'

Miss Collins has told us all about that so I said, 'You
mean the Black Death what killed all them people
hundreds of years ago?' and Pa said, 'Yeah, seems like
it's back again.

Artie who's always asking questions wanted to know
what's it do to you? and Ma said, 'You get fever and
the shakes.'

Pa put on this real scary voice and said, 'And you get
big lumps on your neck and in your armpits, big as eggs,
only black.'

Me and Fred looked at each other and checked our
arms to make sure, only there was nothing.

The paper says it's been in China and India. Now it's
in some place called Noumea Pa says is much closer. And
there's sixteen people got it there already and one dead. I
hope it don't come no nearer but.

Since I got my skipping rope I've been practising
every day and I'm real good now. I can do slow and
peppers and cross-over arms and I've got this new rhyme
that goes

*Over the garden wall*
*I let the baby fall*
*Me mother come out*
*And give me a clout*
*And sent me over the wall.*

Only when Ma heard me she said, 'I'll give you a clout all right, if you don't peel them potatoes like I told you.'

Pa got work today and brung home a bit of mutton for tea. He said he got it real cheap cos the butcher was closing anyway and was only going to throw it out. So Ma boiled it up with the taters and it tasted a bit funny, only not too bad.

Ma can't read or write, only her name, that's why Pa reads to her to tell her what's going on. Last night there was this bit in the paper about some place in Africa called Ladysmith where there's been fighting. Come Christmas Day, and the Boojers shot this shell over the wall into the town only it didn't go off and when the soldiers come over for a geek they found this Christmas pudding stuffed inside. Fair dinkum, with a note saying Happy Christmas and all.

Ma laughed when she heard, only not when Pa read out the bit about Queenslanders fighting at some place called Sunnyside and a trooper's been killed. Ma looked real worried then, what with Bertie going, only Pa said, 'Don't worry, Ma. Bertie can take care of hisself.'

Funny name for a place for fighting. Sunnyside.

Bertie's gone back to barracks now, only we'll get to wave him off when his ship sails.

It's holidays now, not school, and just as well. It's bad enough having to help Ma in the wash house when it's hot, what with all the steam, specially when I got to do the mangling. But stuck in class doing sums'd be worse. I like reading and writing and don't mind sewing which us girls has to do to go into service, only I hate sums. Boys get to do carpentry and Fred says sums'll help him because he wants to be a builder. Artie'll most probably make furniture and Maisie don't know. She only started last year.

Miss Collins says if I work real hard, maybe I can prove to Ma I can do better than domestic. I hope so. When I showed Ma my diary she said, 'What you want to do that for? Don't think you're getting out of service, my girl.' I'm hoping she'll change her mind.

Today but, I had this wonderful idea. I'm going to teach Ma to read and write. I've got my slate and chalk and we can use Pa's newspapers for practice and it'll be our secret, her's and mine. Then she'll be able to read the papers for herself. She'd like that, I'm sure. And won't Pa be surprised!

There's a ship called *Maroc* come in from Noumea, Pa says, only it's stuck over at North Head in quarantine. It'll have to stay there for twelve days with nobody allowed off in case they brung plague with them. Quite right, too. It were 80 degrees again today, not as hot as it can get, but awful humid and with no rain for ages so the gutters and drains are real dirty. Still, as Ma says, at least the clothes get dried and with Pa not getting any work she needs all the sun she can get.

Yesterday, I wrote down all the names in our family on a bit of paper and made Ma copy them on my slate. Then I had her point to the letters and say them out loud. Her name's Pearl and Pa's is William so we got most of the letters between us. There's only the funny ones left. Afterwards we sat and read the adverts together.

Farmer and Company, one of them toff's shops up town, has got ladies' blouses, silk, come all the way from Paris. You can get them in any colour, it says, fancy pink or navy, cardinal and heliotrope—whatever that is—and they got striped silk shirts as well. I told Ma they're probably what Mrs Alexander wears. She's the lady that Mabel works for and whenever Mabel comes to visit on her day off, she's always talking about Mrs Anderson's fancy clobber.

Ma must've been thinking the same, because suddenly she picks up this big pair of lacy drawers from the pile of ironing she got to do and drapes them round her shoulders like.

'How do I look? La-di-da?' she says and dances round and round the kitchen like it was the Federation Waltz almost. But we did laugh.

Then I see this fancy jeweller's ad for Princess pearl clasps on a ribbon as goes round the neck and I says, 'There Ma. That's the latest fashion.'

Ma says, 'Well I never! Fancy that. And all this time I was wondering what was missing from me outfit.'

There was a notice too for a lady typist and shorthand writer and I tell Ma it's what I want to do, only it says office experience necessary. But quick as a flash, Ma says, 'Now, Kitty, you know what I've said about that,' so I don't mention it no more and don't read out the one about respectable girl needed for light housework, neither. Ma don't need to know that. She might make me apply. I just hope by the time she can read by herself she'll have gone off the idea of me being a domestic. At least, I hope so.

Pa says the government's sent off for some medicine that's meant to stop you getting plague. It come all the way from India cos they've had it already and you get it from a needle shoved in your arm. I don't like the sound of that but.

Tiger, the cat as lives round Ferry Lane, chased a rat in our yard today. He had it stuck out the sides of his mouth like he had this big handlebar moustache and looked ever so funny. Only when he brung it in the kitchen and dumped it at Ma's feet for a present like, she screamed and told him to take it outside. Pa threw it over the fence then, into the gutter, and shooed Tiger off home. He says it's the heat that's brung them. If it turned cold tomorrow the rats'd most probably disappear. Not much chance of that but. Pa says the council should do something about the drains, rain or no rain, clean them up proper and get rid of the rats.

Bertie come round to see us this arvo. He says each trooper's
to get at least 4 shillings and 6 pence a day in South Africa.
Ma's jaw dropped when she heard. 'That's a bloomin' fortune
for you,' she says.

Bertie grinned, 'Yeah I know and there won't be nothing to
spend it on except beer and cards.'

Only Ma says, 'You spend that much on beer and cards,
my lad, when there's mouths to feed at home and I'll be on to
you quick smart, I will.'

'Yes Ma,' says Bertie and winks at me. Then he has to
promise Ma he'll get the army to send some of his pay back
to her.

I'll miss Bertie, but he says he'll write to me if I write to
him first. I know he calls me chicken legs on account of I'm
skinny, but he don't really mean it. He only does it to tease,
and besides he says I got real nice eyes. They're greeny and
Bertie says some day they'll get me into trouble, whatever that
means. Bertie's got red hair too, so has Fred, only they both
got Pa's blue eyes.

There's horses for the army gone off to South Africa
already but Pa says some never make it. They die on the way
over if the ship hits bad weather. They get knocked about in
their stalls and when they're hurt real bad, they have to be put
down, on account of its kinder. Then their bodies is pushed
overboard. That's so sad but. There was five lost on Langton
Grange only a while back. I don't think it's fair horses have to
go to war, when it was people started it. Sometimes when they
get there, Pa says, there's not enough feed for them either or
water and they catch diseases like diphtheria, only for horses.

I saw Mr Ah Han today. He had his dray up in Kent
Street. I always stop and pat his horse and let it nuzzle
my hand, just like I used to pat Pa's horse when he had
one. Lots of the kids round here call Mr Ah Han 'Chink'
or 'Chinaman' only Ma says that's rude. Sometimes he
gives me an apple, or maybe a spotty ripe banana, cos I
don't. He always laughs and says I got freckles just like
the banana. I hate my freckles only I don't mind Mr Ah
Han teasing cos he don't mean to be unkind either.

Just because the troopers are going off to fight, it
seems everybody's giving them things. I can't see why
but. There's people giving them horses and presents and
fruit to take with them and there's ever so many dinners
and concerts on. Bertie's been to lots already and the
night before they sail he says they're off to Government
House on the invite of His Excellency. Ma said better him
than her when she heard. She don't have a thing to wear,
only I said, 'But Ma, don't you remember, there's your
heliotrope blouse from Paris and the Princess pearl clasp.'

Ma said, 'Now why didn't think of that?' and we
started to laugh and Bertie and Pa had no idea what we
was talking about!

Pa's real keen on a federation and he says the diggers on the goldfields in West Australia want to vote on it now. And a good thing too Pa says, because West Australia hasn't said yes yet. They say they're too far away from us eastern colonies for it to matter to them and besides, the railway tracks'll be different sizes. But maybe if the diggers vote for it, then the rest of West Australia'll have to change their minds.

Real sticky weather this. Pa went down the wharves today looking for work. The foreman said there was a ship come in as had to be cleaned so Pa said he'd be in it. Only it were so filthy he'd never seen nothing like it. They all got given nips of rum before they went down the hold on account of the smell were so bad they'd've been sick otherwise. Pa said the ship had been stuck out at sea for weeks and weeks and the cargo rotted and the rats got really bad. Anyway when they opened the hatches all these rats come pouring out on the wharf and headed up the hill towards the houses. I shivered when I heard. So did Ma. 'Didn't they have them round things on the ropes as stops them?' she said and Pa said, 'Course. Only so many of the blighters come ashore all at once rat guards was useless. If they fell in the water they just started swimming.'

Fred and Artie said they saw some big ones down Pottinger Street today. They was playing with Elsie Paine as lives in Ferry Lane what owns Tiger. Fred found this bit of tin he wanted to take home to Pa. Only when he lifted it up rats scarpered everywhere and Elsie screamed.

13

Just as well Jess, her little sister, and Maisie weren't there. Fred said it must have been a nest because there was little'ns there as well as big'ns.

The paper says there's this toff Lord Roberts gone off to South Africa to run the war. He's a Field-Marshall and that's as high a soldier as you can get Pa says. Only the Queen's higher and that's cos it's her army. If anyone can win the war and beat the Boojers, he can. It'll probably be over now before we know it, only Bertie won't be pleased if he gets there and finds there's no fighting left. It's sad but Lord Roberts' only son were killed there only last month and he still got to go.

Ma and I did some more reading today. First I read a bit out then Ma says it after and points to the words as she goes. There was this notice that said Mrs Fairfax at her residence Leamington Tintern Road Summer Hill the wife of Charles E Fairfax a daughter. And I said, 'What's all that then?'

Ma said it were just a fancy way of saying she's had a baby. Then she said, 'Come to think of it, I could have had me name in the paper nine times with you lot. "Mrs Barnes at her residence Windmill Street The Rocks." It

makes it sound quite grand don't it, instead of just
another mouth to feed.'

Then I found an advert for Artificial teeth, £2.10s,
perfectly fitted, and I got the giggles, only Ma said all
serious she'd like to be able to buy Pa some of them only
she ain't got the money for frivolities, so he'll just have
to do with the chompers he's got till her ship comes in.

Ma's always talking about when her ship comes in.
She says it's loaded up that much with money now it's a
wonder it don't sink. I know she don't have a ship but,
not really, she's just saying it. Only when I were little I
did and Maisie still does. Sometimes when we're out and
Maisie sees something in a shop window she wants she
says, 'Ma, can I have that? Please? When your ship
comes in?' And Ma only smiles and says, 'We'll see,
Maisie. We'll see.'

### 12th January, Friday

They're selling school books up town at Dymocks, only
when I saw the advert, I turned the page real quick. Ma's
not got money for books and that'll set her thinking about
me leaving school again, so best left well alone I say. It's
not fair when there's plenty of people asking for boys to
wash bottles or deliver leaflets only she never talks about
Fred or Artie earning their keep. Just me.

Pa helps her sometimes taking the washing and
ironing back to people. Ma says she's never known it so
busy as now. It must be the sticky weather. People wear a
shirt till midday maybe, then take it off and put on

another. Anyway today me and Fred helped Pa, then we went on up to Surry Hills to see Ethel in her factory, then on to Dolly's.

Ethel's factory is awful noisy and dirty. Like going to the bootmaker's, only worse. There's this huge room with all this banging going on that nearly deafens you. All these men hammering shoes on lasts. Then there's big machines that smooth the leather whining away as well. Ethel's job's to put laces in the boots and pack them into boxes marked mens' and ladies'. We waved to her from the doorway only we weren't allowed over to talk to her even if she could've heard us above all the din.

Dolly's factory made me feel nearly ill but, what with the smell coming from all these big vats. It's real sweet and sickly on account of it's a jam factory as well as pickles so there's this sugar cooking and fruit that smells too far gone almost. Then there's vinegar as goes to make the pickles that's sharp in yer nose. I were quite glad when it come time to leave. We didn't know which one were Dolly at first on account of they all wear long white aprons and caps as covers their hair. But then we sees her sitting at a table putting labels on jars and soon as she spots us she give us a wave.

## 13th January, Saturday

*The Herald* says the troopers'll come out the gates of Victoria Barracks over in Paddo and march down Oxford into Bourke Street, then into William. Ma says Ethel and Dolly should tell their foremen it's their brother marching next Wednesday and can they please get away in their break and wave him off. They should get a good view from Hyde Park corner she says.

The troopers'll turn down Pitt Street to Bridge then up past the Treasury to Macquarie Street. And that's where Pa says we'll stand, right in front of the Rum Hospital, as Pa calls Sydney Hospital, on account of he says it's how it were paid for. According to him almost everyone drank rum in the early days.

We should get a good view from there before they march round past St Mary's. That's the big catlick church in the city. Ma's a catlick and Pa's a protty dog. St Andrew's is his church. Anyway, we don't talk religion in our house, that way nobody gets to argue. Pa says God's God and He must be awful busy of a Sunday having to get round to all the churches at once.

The troopers'll end up down at Woolloomooloo where their ships'll be waiting. There's three steamships going. *Surrey*, *Moravian* and *Southern Cross*. That's Bertie's.

### 14th January, Sunday

Ma give herself the day off today. She's that tired. She still spent time doing folding but. She says she's been working that long now, she can't just sit and do nothing or she might break down like an old clock and never go again. Besides she thinks the devil finds work for idle hands. I still don't know how the devil'd know Ma's hands were idle but.

I minded Maisie today. I'm teaching her to jump rope.

She's too little to skip proper. I don't mind having to look after her. There's most girls round here got babies or little'ns to mind. You get used to it. Ethel used to mind Mabel and Dolly did me.

## 15th January, Monday

Monday's washday for most. But every day's washday for Ma almost. She does for people she used to know in service. They got lovely things too, some of them, lace edging and lawn that's ever so soft. Not like calico drawers and combis Maisie and me got to wear. Anything delicate like Ma don't put in the copper but washes by hand in the tub. She makes her own soap and all, boiling up the mutton fat with soda and borax and ammonia till it stinks the kitchen out. She says she knows it's pure then and it won't hurt the clothes and that's what her customers want.

Our wash house is a lean-to out the back. The roof's tin so it gets real hot in summer, especially with the steam from the copper. Sheets and pillow slips and shirts get done first, then dirty things, ending up with Pa's old work clothes which are always worst. When he come home after cleaning out that filthy ship she wanted to throw them all out only he said, 'You can't do that, woman, they're me good work clothes.' Sometimes it's that big a wash but, her hands are red raw almost and her nails all ridged and split, so I have to help out just to give her a rest. But she always stands over me to see I do it right. I hate that. I'd rather hang washing out any day. Pa's put

up a line out back, fixed to the fence one end and a post
the other. Sometimes the load's so heavy but, we have to
get another prop just to help hold it up in the middle, to
stop it trailing in the dirt.

Even if I never get to be a lady typist I'm never going
to take in washing. Not if I can help it. Not after I seen
how hard Ma works and what it done to her hands.

### 16th January, Tuesday

Someone in Adelaide's got bubonic the *Herald* says.
Yesterday. It's getting close. The *Formosa* come in with a
man on board, Weppatein or some such, and he's died of
it. And the ship's been in port two months and some of
the crew's upped and left.

Soon as Ma heard she went to the back door and
yelled, 'Fred! Artie! You come in right now and have a
bath,' and Fred said, 'Aw, do we have to?' only she
insisted. She boiled up the water in the copper and Pa
tipped it in the tub and she told them to make sure and
scrub their knees and behind their ears, or she'd come in
and do it herself. Artie started to grizzle a bit only started
scrubbing just in case.

Pa said there's things you can take for plague.
Vitadatio the paper says is s'posed to purify the blood,
only Ma said that's only adverts. Besides, there's nothing
wrong with her blood and she's not about to start taking
things for it now.

Saw Bertie off today. Ma had us all up early and soon as we'd had a bit of bread and dripping and a cup of tea, we set off in our Sunday best for Macquarie Street to make sure of a good pozzy. George come too, the funeral shop let him off for the morning and Fred and Artie were that excited and kept running ahead. I were too, only I had to make sure they didn't get lost in the crowd. There were all these girls in pretty dresses, white with pin-tucking and lace, only my dress were blue and a bit faded on account of it was one of Dolly's cut downs. I was worried Bertie would be ashamed of me only Ma seen the look on my face and said, 'Never you mind what other people got on, it's what's inside a body that counts, my girl, and Bertie he knows that.' So after that I didn't mind so much.

People was ten deep in places, waving hats and hankies, only we stood on this little wall round the hospital for a better view. Behind us some of the nurses and patients come out on the balconies to wave too.

There was lads as climbed up telegraph poles and lamp posts for a better view and soon as we heard the cheering, all this paper come fluttering out the windows of the buildings opposite looking ever so pretty, like snow. I've never seen snow only that's how it must look I reckon.

Out front the band was playing 'Soldiers of the Queen' and Ma said it brung a tear to her eye. They must have heard cos they finished playing that and started on 'Dolly Gray'. That's her favourite and it cheered her up.

Then the officers come riding past and the troopers marching right behind. And suddenly I yell, 'There's

Bertie, Ma! Oooh, don't he look handsome!'

Ma says, 'Shush, Kitty, you'll embarrass him. Where?' Then she shouts out almost as loud, 'Bertie, over 'ere!' and Pa says, 'Good on you, son. You show 'em!' and lifts Maisie up on his shoulders for a better view.

The troopers were all in brown, only Ma says it is khaki, and hard to spot them in Africa, not like red or blue that's easy to shoot. Bertie's tall, taller than Pa even, and with his hat turned up the side and all them feathers stuck up he looked even taller.

They went past in the blink of an eye and we could hear the crowds further on as they went round the corner and down to the wharves.

Ma was a bit teary then, only George said, 'Cheer up, Ma, he'll be back before you know it.' And after that he went back to his coffin shop and we come on home.

### 18th January, Thursday

I felt quite down today. So did Ma. Seeing all them soldiers and hearing all that music she said, it didn't somehow seem fair having to come home and start washing again. But she perked up a bit when Pa come back from the Herald office down Pitt Street. He said they got all these pictures up showing all these little boats out on the harbour seeing them off. Even rowing boats. Fred and me heard the foghorns yesterday and a man that were standing next to Pa told him the band on the wharf went on playing 'Rule Britannia' and 'Auld Lang Syne' till the ships was on their way. I'm really sorry I missed that but.

*Southern Cross* has sent a message back to say thank you for the presents and *Moravia's* gone and let off some carrier pigeons. One come back with a note saying the horses are well, only the other three pigeons got lost in a storm at sea.

### 19th January, Friday

Guess what? Mr Paine, Elsie's pa, has come down with bubonic. That's what Mrs Higgs told Ma. The Paines live in number 10 Ferry Lane and Mrs Higgs is next door. She said he come home sick from work round midday today. (He's a carter down Central Wharf, as drives a lorry with two horses.) He said he felt crook and Mrs Paine thought he were just coming down with flu on account of he had a temperature and aches and pains so she put him to bed.

Ma said, 'Poor Arthur,' when she heard and, 'He's only 35. That's younger than me.' So I asked how old she were and Ma said I were nosey enough to know the ins and outs of a chook's bum. So I shut up after that only I think she's maybe 40 or 41. It seems ever so old, only Ma's short and round so it's hard to tell. Anyway she says we're not to go nowhere near Paines' place or play with Elsie or Jess, and that'll be hard on Artie and Maisie.

Mrs Higgs has told Ma that Arthur Paine got pains in his stomach now and he come on delirious during the night yelling out and all. Mrs Higgs said she heard him on account of the wall's thin between their two houses. The Paines got a bigger house than ours, a two up two downer. The live-in help sleeps out back in a lean-to next the kitchen.

The Premier of Victoria, Mr Deakin, has gone to London to see the Queen. He's going to ask if we can have a federation and she's bound to say yes now we've sent all our troopers off to fight for her. Pa says all the colonies voted for one last year, except West Australia. But that's no reason not to have one just cos they can't make up their minds. Maybe Miss Collins is right and this time next year we'll have a federation.

Guess what? There's been seven stowaways found on board the *Southern Cross!* The oldest's 28 and the youngest only 14. Fancy anyone being that keen to fight a war they'd stow away? You wouldn't catch me doing it but.

**21st January, Sunday**

Nothing special today. Except Reggie Cook says if Mr Paine dies, they'll most probably paint a big red cross on his door and after dark a cart'll come along Ferry Lane and the man'll yell out, 'Bring out yer dead!' like they used to in Black Death time. Only I told Reggie not to be so stupid. It were different now, and besides, he were just trying to give me the heebie-jeebies.

Reggie's pa's a wharfie and ever so big. Reggie says he wants to be strong like him only he's still a bit skinny. When his ma's out he gets her flat irons and does wheelies and windmills with his arms so he'll end up with arms just like his pa's. I can't see no difference yet but, he's got black hair like his pa, so maybe he'll end up with arms like him too.

### 22nd January, Monday

There's been more rats out the backyard and Ma even found one in the wash house eating her good soap. 'You get away from that!' she yelled and got after it with the clothes stick only she didn't catch it.

I said, 'It just goes to show, Ma. He knows it's pure.' Only Ma didn't think that were funny.

Every day now me and Maisie sing

*Ring-a-ring o'rosies,*
*A pocket full of posies*
*A-tishoo! A-tishoo!*
*We all fall down*

ever since Mr Paine come down sick just in case. Ma used to sing it when she were little so it must be really old. It can't do no harm and it's better than nothing.

No news of Mr Paine still. Mrs Higgs said their blinds are down so you can't see nothing to know what's happening. I keep expecting George in his undertaker cart to come round, only he's not been so far.

There's a policeman standing outside the house and he's not letting nobody in or out. All us neighbours want to know how bad it is, only the copper won't say. Reggie dared me go and ask if Mr Paine was going to die but the copper only said, 'It ain't none of your business. Go on, clear out!'

## 24th January, Wednesday

The doctor come again today to Paines, and before you know it there was an ambulance pulled up in Windmill Street. The sides were closed in so you couldn't see nothing, only then Mr Paine come out on a stretcher looking ever so sick. I couldn't see no big black lumps on his neck on account of there was this grey blanket over him, same colour as his face, right up to his chin. Mrs Paine were with him and Elsie and Jess, and Harry the baby, he's 3. Annie French, the help, come out too, then Mr Paine's sister Hannah. She were just visiting to see how he were only the policeman made her stay behind. There was no room in the back of the ambulance for her but, so she sat up top on the seat next the driver.

The horses set off and me and Fred waved just in case

it's the last time we ever see them. It seemed proper somehow. Then the ambulance went down the wharf to the launch waiting to take them over to quarantine. It's only a little boat, green with a black funnel but it gives me the creeps cos Ma calls it the Death Launch. She says them as goes off in it don't always come back. Now I'm really scared. I hope there's no one else comes down with it round here. I keep looking about for people as looks sick or got big black lumps on their necks.

The paper says there was dead rats in Adelaide near where that man died. I hope we don't see any, or more live ones neither. I hate both. They're up in the ceiling of a night and I can hear them scuttling over me head and can't get to sleep for fear they'll drop down on me face and maybe start eating it. Ma says that's nonsense but. They're even scareder of me. She says you does your best to keep things clean but no matter how hard you try there's always rats round somewhere. And Pa says they eat anything, even pigeon droppings, and there's plenty of them on our roof. And they eat Ma's special soap.

### 25th January, Thursday

Paines' things went off today. A cart come down Ferry Lane and pulled up outside their house and two men went in. And next thing they come out with all the mattresses, kapok and straw, and the baby's cot. Then the pillows and shawls, then their cats, three of them, dead. Fred said one were Tiger, so he must have got it too and we stood right back after that.

Even though there's plague about there was still a holiday today on account of it being Anniversary Day. Ma said we had to do something to get us out of the house not sit at home worrying. There's been lots of ads for outings so I showed Pa one for the Zoological Gardens over Moore Park and could we please go there I said on account of they got this wild man from Borneo, an orang-outang, and lots of lions and tigers in cages.

Then Fred says he wants to see the pumas and Artie wants to know what's a puma and Fred said they're lions and tigers only without manes and stripes. And Maisie says she wants a ride on an elephant, only Pa says, 'Shush, the lot of you. What's all this going to set me back?' Then he reads the advert and says, 'It says 6d for adults and 3d for children. How much is that then, quick?' I were just working it out when Fred says, quick as anything, '2 shillings for all of us.'

'That's right,' says Pa, 'well let's see now,' and he pulls out his trouser pockets to show they's empty.

We didn't say nothing then, only Ma gets out her purse to see what she has. 'I ain't got enough for no zoo,' she says, 'but how about we go to the park and stop off first and I buy us a big bag of humbugs?'

We say, 'Yes please, Ma,' cos we like humbugs and they're better'n nothing.

After that we went up Observatory Hill and played chasings and hidings while Ma and Pa sat on a seat looking out over the wharves. It were a good day and we didn't see one rat.

27

The paper today said there were big crowds out yesterday for the holiday so nobody were worried about getting bubonic. Only us as lives near the Paines that is.

There's been a big battle in South Africa Pa says, somewhere called Spinning Top. Least that's what it sounded like only that can't be right can it? Anyway it was up a mountain and the British were on this flat part near the top, only the Boojers were higher up still on the mountains round about. There's more than two hundred dead and wounded or missing and lots left out in the sun all day. The stretcher bearers couldn't get to them fast enough and some of them died while they was waiting to get to hospital.

Bertie weren't there, thank goodness. He's still on his ship going over. He sent us a postcard from Melbourne saying he don't know what happened to all the presents they was s'posed to get. He's not seen any of them. No beer or biscuits or fruit even. Pa says maybe the officers got to them first.

*The Herald* says when his ship got to Adelaide, they all got off and went to the theatre and when Ma heard she said, 'That Bertie's been to the theatre more times in the past month than I have in me whole life.'

Bertie says on board ship they fill in time with boxing matches and Pa said that don't sound to him like Bertie's in the army, sounds more like he's on holiday and if Pa had known he was going to be having such a good time, he would have enlisted himself. Only Ma give him a look and said would he now? and Pa said he were only joking.

Lord Roberts has told his troopers, 'Thou shalt not loot.' I thought that must be the way he talks. Posh. Only Pa says it's probably only the newspaper saying it and his lordship most likely talks normal like us. Put this way but, it sounds like it come from the Bible so maybe the troops'll take more notice. Ma thinks it's dreadful that anyone'd go looting only Pa says people do all sorts of terrible things in war, what they don't do other times.

There's no news of Mr Paine still. I hope Elsie and Jess and little Harry are all right and not come down with it yet.

Some men come round this afternoon to clean out their place. They told Mrs Higgs the government sent them and they was ever so careful. They cleaned all the floors and woodwork with scalding water to get rid of the fleas. I asked Pa why they'd want to get rid of fleas, they're that small they can't hurt you. Only Pa says there's always dead rats round people as has bubonic and rats got fleas and they think now maybe the fleas give it to humans.

### 28th January, Sunday

There's no one else got plague so far, but the coppers been round most houses today saying we all got to go to quarantine tomorrow, on account of we're contacts. And Artie said, 'What's a contact?' and Ma said, 'It's anyone as knows the Paines well enough to maybe have a cup of tea at their place, or works with Mr Paine down the wharf, or plays with Elsie and Jess, so that means me, Fred, Artie and Maisie for starters and Pa and Ma besides.

It's not just us neither, there's lots of neighbours

having to go too. Mrs Higgs and her lot and others round here. All down the end of Pottinger, Windmill and round in Lower Fort as well. Even Mr Ah Han and his family got to go. They live the other side of town in Campbell Street, near Belmore Markets, only the Paines buy vegies from him and Mrs Paine sometimes give him a cup of tea. It's almost the end of his run and he's ready for a chat.

The coppers said we can take clothes and toys and bedding so I'll take my skipping rope BUT NOT my diary, I'm leaving that behind. Tomorrow morning soon as I get up I'll bury it down the backyard wrapped up and hidden where no one'll think to look. That way no one at the station will get to read it, or worse still, take it from me.


### 29th January, Monday


Hardly slept a wink last night I was that scared of what's going to happen to us, and Maisie who shares with me kept tossing and whimpering in her sleep all night. I could hear rats up the roof scratching and skittering round like they was having a party. Sounded like there was hundreds. They're getting more cheeky too. Pa found one this week coming up stairs, bold as you please, like he was toddling off to bed! He killed it of course, only he says there's plenty more where it come from. Now he's put the bed legs in tins of water, but if they can swim ashore it don't seem much point really. Besides they could easy get to us on our mattresses.

Fred and Artie don't say much about it, but I've seen Fred with his arm round Artie so I know they're scared and Ma keeps on packing and unpacking like she's trying to decide what to take. That's her way of pretending she isn't. Pa's worried what'll happen to the house while we're away. And I keep thinking about the launch. If it's true what they say, what if one of us catches it over there and don't come back? I'm going to say Ring-a-ring o'roses every day while I'm over there, just in case.

I were up real early this morning helping Ma and she give me this scrap of sheeting when I asked her. She said what were it for and I didn't want to say, only then Maisie come in the wash house asking could she take her Topsy doll with her that she got for Christmas, so I slipped out back. I'm wrapping up my diary now. They say we'll be allowed back in ten days. I only hope they're right but.

### 9th February, Friday

Dear Diary, we come back home again safe and none of us dead, thank goodness and my diary were right where I left it. The rag kept the dirt out and it didn't rain. Just as well too cos I hadn't thought of that and if it had I'd have come back and found all the pages muddy.

North Head were awful at first, but at least we wasn't the only ones there. The launch kept going backwards and forwards to pick us all up and almost everyone we knew. When we got off this man met us and took all our things off in a handcart along some tracks. I thought we'd never see them again and Pa would try and stop him only he said they were just going for fumigating.

Fred said, 'What's fumigating?' and Pa said it's when

you put everything in a big bath that's full of steam. They reckon it'll kill any plague germs.

Then the man come back for Maisie's Topsy doll and made to grab it only Maisie starts crying and wouldn't let go. He said he had to take it and Ma said sorry lovey, and somehow managed to get it from her. Only Maisie kept hitting Ma, she was that upset, but then Pa picked her up and cuddled her and told her Topsy was only going off for a bath and after that Maisie calmed down a bit.

That's all I've got time for now on account of there's nothing in and Ma says I got to run to the shop to get something for tea. I'll write some more tomorrow.


### 10th February, Saturday


We had sausages for tea last night. Ma said it were nice not having to work out what to feed us of a night and maybe her old stove does cook slow as a wet wash day but it's still good to be back home and all of us safe.

Soon as they took our things away, we had to line up for showers. None of us kids had ever had a shower, just baths in the tub out the wash house, then only once a week on hair-wash night. The rest of the time it's topping and tailing from the jug and basin before we get dressed of a morning.

Artie wanted to see Mr Paine only Ma said he were up in the hospital and no he couldn't see him.

Artie said, 'Why not? I want to see if he got any black lumps yet.'

Ma says, 'It's none of your business what he got. There's only doctors and nurses allowed in to see him and they got to dress proper so as not to catch nothing.'

The shower building give me the creeps. We had to step down inside these boxes, one each, and take off all our unmentionables, only there was a peep-hole for them to spy on us and make sure we did. I got real embarrassed on account of I didn't want nobody seeing me without mine. Then suddenly the water starts coming out real hot, burning almost and Maisie starts screaming and that sets Eddy, Reggie's little brother, off and now all the littlies is yelling their heads off and the matron come along and tell us not to make such a fuss, it were only some phenol they puts in the water.

Ma says, 'Phenol! That takes your skin off.'

Pa says, 'You got no right to use that on kiddies.'

But the lady just says it's for our own good and do we want to catch plague or don't we? And Pa can't say nothing after that.

When we come out but, our skin was all red, raw almost, even Pa. He tried to make us laugh, saying now we weren't the Barnes family we was the Red Apple family, only none of us felt like laughing, our skin were that sore and all the while Maisie wouldn't give over grizzling no matter what.

Most of the neighbours were looking red like us and Mr Ah Han's family all waiting for the matron to bring us clean clothes, ours being damp still. And for once in his life Reggie Cook didn't have nothing to say for hisself. He looked like a tomato, only I didn't laugh because my face were just as sore as his.

I have to stop now, cos Ma's calling me. She wants me to tidy and dust downstairs because Ethel and Dolly and George are coming over tomorrow. I'll write some more after they've gone.

I lay awake last night listening to rats in the ceiling. I'm sure there's more of them since we been away and there's nothing Pa can do about it. He puts out traps every night but only ever catches one or two and what's the use of that when there's so many?

Ma made scones for arvo tea and Dolly brought us some jam. She gets it cheap from her factory, big tins of dark plum, my favourite.

She says her factory's holding a competition for kids to write an essay. Artie wanted to know what an essay was and Dolly told him it meant writing down what you think about something. And Ma said, 'That won't be hard for Kitty. She's always giving me her twopence worth!'

I didn't think that were fair, only then Pa picked up the advert Dolly had cut from the paper and he read: 'My Favourite Occupation. It says here you got to write one page and have it in by 1st of March. You can do that Kitty.'

Then Dolly said you got to have twelve 'O.K' jam tin labels to go with it.

'Well we got them,' says Pa. 'They're still on the tins under the bed legs and there's more out back.'

There's real nice prizes, Dolly says, lady's dressing case in fancy leather and nice hairbrush, comb and mirror, and a manicure set. She says she's seen them in the manager's office. There's prizes for boys too, only Fred hates writing things. He just likes sums and figuring out. I didn't say much, just slipped the advert in me pinny pocket to read later.

Ethel said she and George were worried about us at

North Head, only it don't seem like anyone else in Sydney's worried about plague. At least not over their side of town.

Ma told them it were hard at first but once we settled in and got a bed each, Pa and the boys in one block, us in another and three meals a day it were better. First holiday she'd had in years. She worried about her customers' washing, but there were nothing she could do about it.

Then Maisie piped up, 'They was mean to Topsy,' and straight away she's off and brings back Topsy to show them her face all streaky where the dye's run and now she look more a clown than a dolly. Only George says, 'Poor old Topsy but just think, Maisie, Topsy didn't get sick, did she and you neither and that's good isn't it?' and Maisie frowned like she was still cross only thinking about it, then she run off to play. I didn't say nothing only just as well I didn't take my diary, or it've been ruined for sure.

Artie told them they give us a needle in the arm too and George says, 'Did you cry mate?' And Artie says, 'Nope!' So George ruffles his hair and says, 'Good on yer.' There's no way I would have cried, not in front of Reggie Cook, no matter how much it hurt.

It's school again tomorrow, worst luck. It started last Monday and Pa says we got to go back even if it is a week late.

### 12th February, Monday

School weren't too bad today, apart from sums. Miss Collins were real pleased to see us and asked how my diary was going. I told her I write something every day almost, only not while we were away. Then I told how I'd hidden it in the backyard and she laughed and said that were smart of me. Miss Collins ain't much bigger than me, only she's real pretty with browny curly hair and big eyes, blue like she's surprised. She's ever so smart too.

She got this idea we should make things for sick soldiers. She says girls at Cleveland Street School been making pyjamas and caps and cholera belts and would we like to? I told her our Bertie had gone off to fight the Boers and she says, 'Has he now? Well then, that settles it.' I think I can make pyjamas and caps all right, but what's she mean by a cholera belt I wonder.

Pa went out to find himself a *Herald* this evening and come back with Saturday's as well. He settled down with them and said that were what he missed most about quarantine, not being able to keep up with the news that was happening outside.

*The Herald* says Mr Edmund Barton's gone off with Mr Deakin and others to tell England why we want a federation. Pa says Barton's a good chap and he wouldn't mind seeing him made prime minister only I said, 'Reggie Cook calls him Toby Tosspot.'

Straight away Ma's on to me, 'You wash your mouth out with soap and water, my girl. Fancy **saying** things like that!'

Only Pa says I'm right. It is his nickname, only all it means is he's fond of his food and likes a glass of wine to go with it. It don't mean he's not a good man, Pa says, and in the parliament Mr Barton's the only one of them that keeps calm all the time.

## 13th February, Tuesday

It's funny being back at school, specially when all we did
at North Head was play, even if it did mean Reggie and
me having to mind Eddy and Maisie all the time. There
was all this room to run round and lots of good places to
hide. And some of the roads up top were perfect for
skipping so I taught Soo and Li to skip.

Ma spent her time sewing. Shrouds, mostly. It give
me the shudders like they was waiting for all these people
to die, only Ma said they give her a choice between that
or laundry and Ma said, 'Not on your Nelly,' to laundry.

I've been thinking what I can write for my essay.
Other kids, rich ones specially, will probably say their
favourite occupation is riding their pony or bicycle
maybe. But I ain't got either so I'm going to write my
favourite occupation is keeping my diary. And it is, I've
decided, even more than skipping.

## 14th February, Wednesday

Ma and me are back reading again now that Pa's started
bringing home the paper regular. Not when he's around
but. It's still meant to be a surprise. We practise soon as I
get home after school and before she has to get tea. There
was an advert in today for Keating's Insect Powder that's
meant to kill fleas and I asked why they didn't use that in
Paine's house, only she said scalding water was cheaper
and just imagine how many tins of Keatings you'd need

to do a whole house? Ma thinks they should knock down a lot of the houses round here. Should have done years ago. Get rid of the damp and rot, too she says.

Today when I come home from school I found this note addressed to me.

> *Kitty Barnes will you be mine*
> *Just to call my Valentine.*

It was signed 'An Admirer' only I know it come from Reggie Cook, on account of I seen him slip it through the letter-slit in the door just as I come over the hill. Then he shot back inside his own door.

## 15th February, Thursday

No sign of Reggie today. Maybe he's sorry he sent it? He don't go to our school. He goes to St Joseph's up Lower Fort Street and gets home before we do. I've not said I know it's him that sent it. That'd be too bold. I'll just keep him guessing. I like Reggie, only he's a bit keen on hisself. He's got nice eyes but. Brown.

Kimberley's been relieved Pa says. That's a town in Africa where Mr Cecil Rhodes has his diamond mines. And the Boers have had it surrounded for a hundred and twenty-four days. Fancy not being able to get out all that time. A bit like the copper standing in front of Paines' house, only worse. Anyway, Major-General French come riding in and saved it and he had Australian troopers with him. The saddest thing but, was all the horses that died on the way in. Pa said it took seventy-five miles to get there and they had hardly any feed or water all that time.

## 16th February, Friday

I'm always on the lookout now for rats. Dead or alive. Specially round the WC. Our privy's down the bottom of the yard. That sounds funny our WC being at the bottom of something. Anyway the door creaks so everyone knows you've gone in the bog and it don't shut neither so sometimes when you go to push it Pa yells out, 'Hey! I were here first!'

There's all these spiders' webs up in the corners like dirty lace and me and Maisie try to get out fast as we can, specially at night when it's dark and you have to feel about on the floor for the pile of torn up *Heralds* Ma's put there for bum paper. One night, when they first moved in, Ma sat on a neighbour's chook that were sitting on the seat. She weren't sure who got the bigger fright, her or the chook. It took off over the fence squawking its head off and never come back, only Ma says now she always checks the seat first to see there's no chook there.

Saw Reggie over the other side of the road today and pretended I didn't see him only then he give me a wave so I had to wave back.

## 17th February, Saturday

Bertie must be just about in Africa by now. The paper says the 2nd Contingent were due to arrive today only Pa says they probably won't let them off till Monday. Artie said

why not, didn't they let you fight on Saturdays and
Sundays? And Pa said of course they do, only if they let the
troopers off on a Saturday arvo they might not come back
again till Monday. They might not come back at all! Then
Ma bung on this posh voice and said, 'Yeah they's most
probably decided to take themselves off to the the-ater!'

### 18th February, Sunday

The Paines come back again yesterday. Mr Paine too.
Seems he's better now. But they found their house all
covered in lime. Mrs Higgs had made them a stew to
make up a bit and Ma left a plate of scones for them, only
it must have been a shock to find it looking like that.
   Reggie were at Mass today with his Ma and he give
me a wink across the aisle only I lowered me eyes and
pretended I were saying prayers.

### 19th February, Monday

Bertie must have landed by now and I'll bet he's all
excited. Pa says they got twenty officers and three
hundred troopers and more than four hundred horses.
Bertie's in the NSW Mounted Rifles. That's part of the
2nd Contingent. But just cos they got horses don't mean
they ride all the time, only from place to place, then they
get off and fight while somebody holds the horses for
them. Pa says it's usually a bugler or drummer that's too

young to fight. I expect it's what that 14-year-old stowaway's doing right now. That's if they haven't sent him back home.

### 20th February, Tuesday

There's a man called Mr Oliver whose job it is to find somewhere for capital city for when we get a federation. He goes round all these different places to look. I can't see why we need a capital city when we got Sydney. Only Pa says people in Melbourne'd say what's wrong with having Melbourne and they'll never agree. So they got to find a new place. Mr Oliver's already seen lots of places like Eden and Goulburn, only he hasn't found one he likes yet.

### 21st February, Wednesday

The trouble with getting Ma to read out adverts is having Maisie listen in. Fred and Artie go out and play in the street, only, Maisie, if she's not with Elsie and Jess, hangs round here. So there's me reading out things for sale and Maisie says can she have a pony that's for sale.

Ma says, 'Lord save me, child! Where would I put a pony?'

Maisie says, 'In the yard.'

'A yard that size?' says Ma. 'With my clean washing?' and that seems to shut her up for a bit till she hears there's someone over Glebe way got a St Bernard for sale.

41

'Then can I have a puppy?' she says. 'That's not as big as a pony so it won't take up as much room.' She even tries to win Ma over by saying it's named after a saint which must make it good.

Only Ma says, 'Maisie, it's hard enough having to feed you lot without feeding a dog or horse besides.' And then she give up and went to play with Topsy.

### 22nd February, Thursday

Elsie and Jess come over to play today after school. Them and Maisie pretended they was fairies out back and Ma tore up an old sheet into triangle rags for wings and pinned them to the back of their pinnies with safety pins. That kept them happy for ages and meant Ma and me could get on with her reading practice. She's getting real good now.

But the best news is tonight I started writing my essay!

### 23rd February, Friday

Ma's getting a bit too good at reading, if you ask me. Seems she's been practising while I've been at school, when she sits down to take the weight off her feet and have a cup of tea. Today when I get in she says, 'You didn't tell me there's been all these adverts for girls needed.'

And I says all innocent like, 'What girls?'

And she says, 'You know very well what girls I mean. Them as wanted for general housemaid or light housework or maybe mind children. You could do any of those, Kitty, but you never said.'

So I think quick and tell her that if she puts me into service now, then I won't be around to help do the mangling and it'll be ages before Maisie's strong enough to work it. Ma thinks about this for a bit, then says, 'Well maybe just a bit longer.' Only I'm thirteen in May remember and she'll see about it after that. So I've still got a bit of time up me sleeve to make her change her mind.

### 24th February, Saturday

There's someone's DIED of bubonic. Captain Thomas Dudley as owns a chandler's shop down Sussex Street. He found five dead rats in a toilet out the back of his shop. Only last Sunday he come down sick and died Thursday in his house over Drummoyne way. Now there's coppers standing guard outside, front and back, and Pa says his body's been taken to North Head where it'll be buried deep down still wrapped up and in its coffin and no one's allowed touch it. His wife and family's gone off to quarantine too and all those as worked alongside him or lived close by.

Most everyone round here knew him but. And us kids used to call him Cannibal Tom on account of Reggie says he was shipwrecked once and him and another man killed a cabin boy and ate him. Fair dinkum! He even went to prison for it, only they let him out after a bit, then he left England

and come out here to live. Fred and Artie and Eddy used to keep right away from him but, just in case.

There's proclamations going up now on the walls round here saying

*Plague is present in Sydney.*
*It has been introduced by diseased rats and there is great danger of its spreading still further.*

They say anyone as finds any sick or dead rats is to tell the Board of Health straight away. They're going to put stuff in the water to flush out the sewers. And about time too Pa says.

Mr Ah Han says there's even been proclamations go up over his way, only they're in Chinese.

There's definitely something been killing the rats down the wharves cos there's lots more of them dead lately. I'm real glad I had that needle. I only hope it works.


### 25th February, Sunday


This morning Ma took Maisie and the boys off to Mass. She said the more prayers Sydney had said for it, the better.

While she was gone but, Pa and me sat down at the kitchen table and he got out the inkwell and some paper and said I was to write a practice essay while he wrote a letter.

So I wrote that keeping a diary's like having a special friend you can write to only you can't see them but. Still that don't matter cos you can tell this friend anything as happens to you and your family, even outside your house. Then I said this was going to be a special year for keeping a diary on account of I could tell my friend all about us getting a federation and how one day if I maybe have children and grandchildren even I can let them read my diary to see what it were like in 1900.

When I'd finished Pa said it were very good only I should maybe check up on some words in my speller at school before writing it out proper. And tomorrow he says he'll buy us two penny stamps from the post office in Millers Street.

### 26th February, Monday

Pa's letter was to the Council Clerk at Town Hall about the rats. He said as how Tiger brung just one in that time only now there's tunnels all under the backyard and it don't matter how many you kill there's always more come in their place. He said we seen them on the stairs and up the bedrooms even. Pa don't know if he'll get an answer. There's probably that many letters come in from other people that got rats too, but they got to do something about it soon or there'll be plague all over Sydney.

There's another person sick now. John Makins as worked for a steamship company in Sussex Street come down with a lump under his arm and stomach pains. Now he's got very high temperature as well and delirious. Sounds to me like he's got it all right.

Today I checked the words for my essay in my speller and after Fred and Artie and Maisie had gone to bed, I sat up for a bit and wrote out my essay on a clean bit of paper Pa give me, in my very best running writing.

Then, soon as I'd blotted the ink and folded the paper

like, I put it in the envelope with the jam tin labels Ma
had got off the tins while I were at school. Then I
addressed it to Peacock's 'O.K.' Jam Co., Broughton
Street, Glebe and Pa give me the penny stamp to put on.

### 27th February, Tuesday

Posted Pa's letter and my essay on the way to school today
and I told Miss Collins about my essay and she were real
pleased. Now all I got to do is cross my fingers and wait.

Saw Reggie after school and told him about the
competition. Only he said if he went in it he'd most
probably win and that wouldn't be fair to me. I were so
cross I told him it were a wonder he didn't send hisself a
Valentine's note. Only then I see him grinning so he
knows I got it. Worst luck. He's the last person I'd have
for a Valentine.

### 28th February, Wednesday

It's Bertie's birthday today only I don't s'pose you're
allowed to have birthdays in the army. He's lucky he weren't
born on the 29th of February cos then he'd only have one
every leap year. I can't remember for leap years if you say 4
goes into it or 8 only Fred says for the end of a century you
got to divide by 400 and that don't go into 1900.

## 1st March, Thursday

Now Ladysmith's been relieved. Yesterday. The Boojers
had it under siege for a hundred and eighteen days. Like
being stuck in quarantine only for longer but. *The Herald*
says when the troopers rode in the people give three
cheers for Queen Victoria and all the church bells started
ringing. I asked Pa why they cheered the Queen and he
says it's because it's her army.

Mr Oliver's been to Marulan now and says it won't
do for a capital city.

## 2nd March, Friday

There's people starting to leave Sydney now. For the Blue
Mountains mostly, but Melbourne too. Ethel come over
for tea tonight and said they was lining up to buy tickets
at Redfern Station this morning. And Mabel's sent a note
saying her 'family''s taking her to the Blue Mountains
where they got another house just to get away from the
city. Ma says all we can do but, is stay put.

Mr Oliver don't like Wingello neither but I expect
he'll find somewhere eventually.

There's another proclamation gone up this morning:
*Bounty 2d a head.*
*For every rat delivered (dead or alive) to*
*the Bathurst Street Public Incinerator.*
*By Order—Board of Health.*

Fred and Artie were that excited when they read it
only they made me promise not to say anything to Ma on
account of they were planning something. I told them not
to go doing something silly but, only then I forgot all
about it and when they weren't around, just thought they
was out playing.

It were only when it started to get late and Ma said to
go and call them and they was nowhere to be seen I
remembered the notice. Then I began to worry where
they'd got to. Only next thing there they were coming
down the hill grinning from ear to ear like they've just
robbed the Bank of New South Wales. Ma took one look
at them and said, 'And what you two been up to then?'

They wouldn't say at first, only they was so pleased
with theirselves, it all started to come out. Seems they'd
found a couple of sacks and went down the wharf and
picked up all the rats they could find, twenty-seven
between them. Artie went mainly for dead'ns on account
of he's not as fast as Fred but Fred had a couple of live
ones in his sack as well. Then bold as brass, they took
them right up town to Bathurst Street incinerator on the
public tram! They said they'd 'borrowed' a couple of
pennies from Ma's purse for their fare up George Street.

Ma's jaw dropped at first, but not for long. She made them empty their pockets and between them they got 4 shillings and 2d left. They'd had 4/6d, only there was the fare back and they bought two bags of boiled lollies on the way home. They wouldn't say why they did it at first, only Ma got it out of them eventually. Seems they wanted to buy her a present for her birthday come end of March.

Anyway, Ma took the twopence and said it were going straight back in her purse, then she marched them straight out the wash house and made them scrub themselves from head to toe before she let them inside again. She told Pa she didn't know whether to laugh or cry. But when she give them their tea Pa said, 'Now you listen to me you two. You're not s'posed to go picking up dead rats just where you find them and take them off for burning. You're meant to soak them in acid first or boiling water to kill all the fleas. You know you could have left fleas on them trams? The pair of you's probably given plague to half of Sydney by now.'

Fred and Artie looked real worried then and Artie said, 'Will that mean the coppers find out and put us in jail?' And Pa said, 'More than likely.' Only then I see him wink at Ma behind their backs and he said all serious like, 'Let's just hope it don't come to that.'

### 4th March, Sunday

Pa was only kidding about Fred and Artie but there's more people starting to come down with it. Now a man named Walker got it in Annandale and someone in Sussex

Street. It's getting really scary. I keep wondering where it'll turn up next. Pa says he's not the least bit surprised about Sussex, and Clarence Street would be just as bad. There's boarding houses down there he says, nothing like Ethel and Dolly's but, where the men are just packed in. Sailors and wharfies mostly, sometimes maybe seventy men all crammed into six rooms. So of course it's going to spread.

There's houses starting to be empty now and put up for sale. All over Sydney just about. Newtown, Stanmore, Enmore out that way and as far as Dulwich Hill and over the east side at Darlinghurst and Darling Point. Maisie saw an advert for one house in Paddington at 75 Cascade Street, as had a loft and stables and that'd mean room for a pony only Pa said, 'It would and all, lovey, if I could afford the pony, let alone the house.'

Yesterday I spent all day helping Ma with the wash. She lost some customers when she were away. They'd found someone else. Now she wants to make up to the others. Once it's been in the copper, she lifts the load out with the wash stick straight into the tub for rinsing. Then she gets me to feed the sheets and pillow slips through the mangle to get rid of the water. It's hard work turning the handle and sometimes I get Fred to give it a few turns while I have a rest. I tell him it'll give him big strong arms like a wharfie one day. Only you have to watch him real careful like, because if a shirt go through with the sheets the buttons get broken in the rollers and then Ma has to sew on new ones and that makes her real cranky.

## 5th March, Monday

There's businesses coming up for sale now and Pa says
there'll be lots of people ruined because of plague.
There's some people won't go near someone that's had it,
or their family or someone that works for them. So
there's all these adverts for butter runs, restaurants,
mercery shops even, all going real cheap.

Still hot and sticky with no sign of a let up yet.
Wonder what it's like up the mountains where Mabel is?
It's been two years since she went into service and I still
miss her. Ethel and Dolly were that bit older to play with
and Maisie's too little really but me and Mabel used to
play together all the time when she were still home. We'd
dress up in Ma's clothes when she let us and sometimes
when she were out in things that belonged to her
customers. Only we had to be ever so careful not to tear
anything as didn't belong to us. One day but Maisie saw
us and told Ma who got that mad we weren't allowed to
touch nothing from the ironing ever again. I bet Mabel
don't go dressing up in Mrs Alexander's things now but.

Seems Mr Oliver don't like Albury for a capital
site neither.

## 6th March, Tuesday

There's more coming down sick now. A family named
Dovey as lives over Moore Park near the rubbish tip and
others besides. And there's been government men round

to inspect all the houses round and yards and water closets. They're going to disinfect everything and Ma says good, it'll save her having to do it and besides, that way, they pay for the carbolic.

### 7th March, Wednesday

That man from Sussex Street died Monday and Mr Walker from Annandale snuffed it yesterday. I'll bet all them shrouds Ma and the others made at North Head are coming in real handy now.

I've not seen Reggie now for a week. Thank heavens.

### 8th March, Thursday

Bertie were in a battle yesterday, at a place called Poplar Grove. Banjo Paterson, the man that wrote 'Waltzing Matilda', is in South Africa writing war things for the *Herald* and he says there was mounted rifles fighting, so that must mean Bertie was there. There were five killed and fifty wounded and soon as Ma heard she crossed herself and said a prayer under her breath only Pa said, 'Now Ma, they would have said if it were Bertie.'

They was meant to circle round and capture the Boers and Mr Kruger, their President, in the middle. Only the Boers took off and got clean away. Pa says our horses were probably too tired to chase them and what can you expect if they only get half rations?

The firing was heavy but and one of the troopers as used to be a copper at Darlinghurst police station, run out in the thick of it to pick up this wounded trooper on the ground and carried him nearly a mile till he were safe.

Later on but, he goes off with this mate looking for Boers and they get off their horses and tie them up, only when they come back they're gone. So then they up and help themselves to a couple of real nice horses tied up in camp. Trouble is, these belong to Lord Roberts hisself so the troopers get arrested and court-martialled, only Lord Roberts lets them off. I'm real glad it weren't Bertie what nicked his lordship's horse.

### 9th March, Friday

They're setting up barricades in Kent Street and others and nobody'll be allowed in or out. Ma came home mad as a bandicoot when she heard. Seems she'd been talking to Mrs Higgs and Mr Higgs won't be able to get out to his job as storeman in a warehouse up town. And Ma said, 'How's anyone s'posed to feed a family with no money coming in?'

Then Artie wanted to know if that meant he didn't have to go to school no more, only Ma said it meant nothing of the sort and he and Fred and Maisie and me'd keep going to school till she said. And Artie said, 'Aw Ma,' but under his breath cos he could see how cross she were.

## 10th March, Saturday

Pa and Mr Higgs and Mr Paine and others are going up Macquarie Street Monday to see Mr Hughes. He's the member of parliament for Rocks. All the grown-ups round are worried what's going to happen if they can't get work and no money coming in.

We had rabbit stew for tea last night, only Ma says there won't be much of that or anything else for that matter if she don't get no washing to do and Pa got no work neither. We'll be living on thin air she says and that's for sure. Then Maisie wanted to know how you could live on air but Ma told her to shush up. She'd find out soon enough.

There's a boy from Redfern got it now, 16, and the Dovey's baby, Frederick's died of it. Only 2. They took him to Sydney Hospital. Now the hospital's closed and nobody can visit and all the Dovey family's gone off to quarantine.

## 11th March, Sunday

Ma and me caught up with the ironing this arvo. Just in case she don't get no work when barricades go up. She heats the flat irons next the stove so one's heating while the other's cooling down. I sprinkle everything with water so the creases come out then she irons and once it's all aired I fold it neat into piles for Pa to deliver. After a day's ironing Ma's arms are worn out. The irons are real heavy. Maisie can hardly lift them but you still got to press down to make them work. Ma's got strong arms, only not like a wharfie's but then she don't do wheelies and windmills with her irons neither.

Pa went up to the Herald building today to read the latest news from South Africa. There's Mounted Rifles been fighting somewhere called Driefontein and a trooper named Abrahams killed. Bertie probably knew him too. It were sad, Pa said. He were shot from a Boer farmhouse flying a white flag to show they'd surrendered. That's cheating but. Then they checked his pockets. They found a letter from his ma he got that morning and hadn't had time to read. I hope they buried it with him. Pa said he were just nineteen, younger than Bertie even.

I've written a letter to Bertie and told him all about our time at North Head and about being back at school again and how there's talk of cleaning up all the streets round here and getting rid of the rats and all. He won't have got it yet but.

Mr Oliver's been to Orange and seen that for a capital city. And Moore Park tip's been closed.

**13th March, Tuesday**

Pa and the other men saw Mr Hughes today. They waited outside Parliament House and demanded to see him till, in the end, some guard went and got him. Mr Hughes were in the middle of this big argument with the Premier, Mr Lyne, about the Rocks and said it's Mr Lyne wants to put barricades up and send in clean-up gangs. Only Mr Hughes told him it weren't fair to people with jobs outside. All they can do now is wait.

All over Sydney there's talk of cleaning up, in Annandale, out Vaucluse way, even over in Manly.

### 14th March, Wednesday

The barricades went up this morning real early before anyone was up and there's a curfew put on anyone that really has to go out to get back before dark. Ma said, 'What we going to do if you can't get out to look for work and I can't get out to pick up my washing?'

And later on, Mr Hughes hisself come round to see Pa and the others. All these people are shouting at him and Mr Hughes, who's real little, has to shout to get heard above the din. Seems he's told Mr Lyne to pay 6 shillings a day to them as can't get out, only so far Mr Lyne's said no. All he'll do is go see the rats for hisself, if they're as bad as Mr Hughes says. Not from close up but, from a boat out on the water.

There's a notice gone up now about stray dogs. Any seen'll be put down painless. Maybe they're worried about dogs' fleas now?

Anthony Hordern, the big toff shop up Brickfield Hill, got this sale on for mourning black. Must be a lot of people expecting to go to funerals. People round here just wear what they got.

There's been rats found in street sweepings way out at Wentworthville and Ma said, 'Fancy that! Rats in the sweepings. They should come over here and see how many we got.' Mr Lyne now says we do have a rat problem. Only we could have told him that. He saw thousands running up and down the wharf piles and swarming all over. Fair makes me flesh crawl to think of it.

There were a riot down Bates Lane this morning when Mr Lyne sent his clean-up gang in from outside, without so much as a by your leave and they start pouring lime all over a cottage. The people as lived there got real angry and a scuffle broke out and all the neighbours joined in. Only it must have got back to parliament because Mr Hughes has made the Premier promise there'll be jobs on gangs for all the men round here, not just from outside. And they'll get paid 8 shillings a day so Pa and Mr Higgs and Mr Paine and anybody that wants can have a job. Elsie's and Reggie's pas can't work since the wharves all closed, so they'll be joining. And Pa's that pleased to be working again, he's got this grin on his face, ear to ear, like his head's split.

Now but, Ma's got no work. None of her old customers want her doing their wash since barricades gone up. Only Ma just shrugged and said it were Pa's turn to bring in some money for a change and she don't mind who does it, so long as someone does.

The paper says New South Mounteds done splendid service trying to capture a Boer gun. They didn't get the gun but the *Herald* said it were a gallant attempt all the same.

Another Dovey's come down with bubonic now, the boy, 7. That makes it four in that family's had it so far.

## 16th March, Friday

Pa says there's something been killing all the fish lately, thousands of them are floating on the surface, bream and mullet, whiting, even flathead. It can't be plague that's killed them but, cos fish don't have fleas do they?

If they put the capital city in Monaro, they could have a harbour at Twofold Bay and a train going there and back. But Pa says it'll mean buying all the land between from the farmers and that'll cost more even than Ma's got on her ship.

When you read about people getting plague and they got names and how old they are it makes it seem like you know them almost. Now just two more today and one yesterday. Today there's a John Butler, 24, who's got it and an Alexander Bell, 18. That's the same age as Ethel.

## 17th March, Saturday

It was St Patrick's Day today and Ma said it's a pity he's not still around. If he could get rid of the snakes out of Ireland, then maybe he could do something about the rats in Sydney.

Lord Roberts has captured Bloemfontein. The paper says the crowds when he led the army in were that excited they ran a white flag up and the Mayor gave him the keys to the town. Only the paper said the men were done in. They'd been marching a whole month on short rations and no tents. It's boiling hot of a day and freezing at nights, and they got wet through when it rained. Ma's hopping mad about it. She says she's never heard of an army this bad organised, that one of them fancy ladies' committees could have done better and would have. At this rate she says Bertie'll be nothing more'n a scarecrow when he gets back and she'll have her hands full just nursing him back to normal.

Lord Roberts says there's not much fighting left to do now, only President Kruger don't agree. He says the burghers, that's what Boer men are called, will fight to the death and the British'll never get as far as Pretoria. Ma said we'll see about that.

### 18th March, Sunday

Dolly's birthday today. She's 17 and taller now than Ethel.

Saw Reggie and his parents at Mass and got to say hello after. He were real nice and polite and didn't sound up hisself at all. In fact on the way back he held Eddy and Maisie's hand and swung their arms forwards and back like a game till they tell him to stop.

Pa met George today in Kent Street with his black cart.
He says they're run off their feet at the coffin shop, not
just from plague neither. There's old people dropping off
the perch with the heat and their hearts giving in and
apoplexy. Only now there's bubonic as well and George
says he's never known it this busy. But he says none of
his friends'll see him, on account of he's round bodies all
day long, and they think he'll maybe pass something on.
Even Lily, the girl he's been stepping out with, won't
have nothing to do with him, which is sad.

George says there's doctors and nurses getting the
same. People are scared they'll catch something now the
hospitals are full. One doctor George knows, every time
he walks along the street with his black bag, people stand
back against the wall to let him pass or else step off on
the road.

**20th March, Tuesday**

There's plague victims popping up all over Sydney now.
Paddington and Surry Hills. Not all dead mind, but catched
it. Marrickville and Burwood, even over Canterbury and as
far down as Botany. And it's not just poor parts either.
There's just as likely to be bad privies over Milson's Point
and Kirribilli as there are this side of the harbour.

Pa says it's become real nasty down the markets.
People are saying the Chinese brung the plague in and it's

all their fault. But that's not fair. The rats brung it. Poor Mr Ah Han hasn't been round for ages now and Pa says coppers have gone up China Town and barricaded people in proper and they're not allowed out at all. He says it's because they won't have needles like us. Mr Ah Han and his family did in quarantine but his neighbours haven't. It's not their sort of medicine so they're frightened.

**22nd March, Thursday**

Two more deaths today and a crowd of people stormed up the Health Department in Macquarie Street to get their needles. Right out across the pavement they were and the doctors tried to keep them out only they kept demanding them same as the people at North Head. The doctors ended up giving a thousand people needles which makes more than three thousand's had them so far, only the doctors say they can't give them in the office any more. They'll have to find somewhere else.

**23rd March, Friday**

They've set up a needle place in Prince Alfred Park. The Exhibition Building, and Ethel and Dolly got theirs today. George's had his already on account of he's dealing with bodies all day. There was twelve hundred got them today and Dolly said they waited in line for ages with their sleeves rolled till they got to the doctor.

There's lots of people haven't had them but, and just

as many left the city, if they haven't died already. Any
houses that's got plague they put a fence right round,
outside its own and onto the roadway so people got to
walk right round the outside. And there's notices gone up
everywhere saying what streets is to be cleaned from
Darling Harbour up Kent and Erskine and along Sussex,
then street by street almost to Waterloo. Down the bottom
the Premier's put his name, William John Lyne, then
GOD SAVE THE QUEEN! I can't think why but. How's
she going to catch it in England?

## 24th March, Saturday

There's a thousand men on clean-up now and Reggie's
fibbed and told them he's 16 so's he's on a gang with his
dad. It's not just clean-up either, they're pulling down
houses as well. The noise all day is something terrible,
what with sledge hammers banging and walls crashing
down. And carts and wagons rumbling down the wharf
the whole time and steam engines spraying the walls and
yards. Fire engines are parked in Kent Street every day
now and there's big hoses lying all over the road. Every
now and then they start blasting. The public still goes
about their business the other side of the barricades but,
while the men clean up our side.

Another one, over in Balmain this time.

The people in Albury are cranky that Mr Oliver didn't
choose there for a capital city. They say they've got a
nice river and soil and even a butter factory. But you
don't have to have a butter factory, do you?

Ragged School's been closed for a week now. All the schools round have. That's how Reggie got on clean-up. All the wharves and warehouses and factories are closed too. It's funny Ma and Ethel and Dolly got no jobs, but George and Pa never worked so hard.

Dolly and Ethel come to the barricades to see us today. They say Sydney's a ghost town further up with lots of places shuttered up. Theatres and hotels, shops and markets are just not opening for a while. Ethel says it's like Sunday only all the time. There's no word from Mabel. I expect she's up the Blue Mountains still.

Ma says me and Maisie got to stay indoors more now, keep out the way of the gangs, only she can't stop Fred and Artie. They're used to being out and about and barefoot too, only now she makes them wear their boots, on account of they're out and about with the rat-catchers. Some places that gets opened up, rats shoot out like mice from a barn and no time to see where they went almost.

Fred and Artie come home so excited first day. They said the men got baits and cages with cats and ferrets. Only the foxies were best and Maisie said, 'What foxies?' And Fred said fox-terriers and Artie said Jack Russells. Catchers keep them on leads till they're ready. Then soon as they let them off, they're down the drains before you can blink and next thing, they're struggling back out with a huge rat, maybe half as big as themselves. Artie said the catchers say there's tunnels pretty well under every backyard like a honeycomb. That give Ma and me the shudders just to think of it. I've got to finish now and go to bed, the noise starts that early of a morning and I'm dog tired.

No one knows if their house is coming down or just getting cleaned. Gangs come into a street, nose round, and next thing, the roof's off and the walls are left standing pink and blue, like their unwhisperables. Some got pictures pasted on or stencils to make them look nice only it's like going into a stranger's house without being asked still. It's odd but, before a house come down, there's a man goes round and takes its picture first. I can't think why he wants a picture of it if it's coming down anyway. Still it don't matter on account of sometimes me and Maisie get to get in the picture too and most of the kids round here do, on account of we've never had our picture taken before.

Only yesterday I'm standing there waiting for him to take it and suddenly I hears someone yelling, 'Kitty. Kitty! Hey, Carrot Top!' and I turn and look just as the flash goes. And there's Reggie, coming over to say hello. He said he couldn't help seeing the red hair. I were that cross because now the photo'll have me with me face all blurred on account of him. And I told him so and he said he were sorry, only he just wanted to say hello but.

Maisie and me got to be ever so careful where we walk now. My boots are almost through and there's that much broken bricks and nails about you could easily get something sticking in. Maisie's the same. She's almost out the end of her boots now. Artie's old ones are still too big on her so she's got to make do for a bit longer.

When you go out, there's this smell all the time. Ma says it's carbolic they're using to disinfect everything and limewash for painting the walls and WCs. Only now it's mixed with privy smell and dead rats and meat gone off and it fair makes you feel like chucking up.

I'm still cross with Reggie Cook for making me photo blurred.

### 28th March, Wednesday

Ma read that Mr Barton and Mr Deakin and them got to have lunch at Windsor Castle and meet the Queen and Ma said, 'Maybe they should ask her where she thinks we should put the capital city.'

There's been more people come down with it now. Over Darlington and Glebe.

### 29th March, Thursday

Something happened today that give me a terrible fright. I had this gut ache and next thing I think I've wet me drawers. So I go down the back to the privy. Only I find there's blood on them and I get such a shock I think I'm dying, that somehow I've come down with bubonic even with the needle. And next thing I'll have black lumps on me neck and fever and the shakes and I'll come on delirious and then the whole family'll get it.

I sit there for a bit, scared stiff and shaking, not knowing what to do I'm that upset. I think of burying them somewhere only Ma will want to know what happened to them so I got to wash it off before she finds out. So I open the door real careful so's it don't creak and run across to the wash house.

And I'm standing there scrubbing me drawers with Ma's special soap, only the blood won't come out and now I'm starting to feel hot and I'm sure it's fever starting and suddenly there's Ma standing behind me.

'Here, what you doing?' she says and I burst into tears.

'I've got bubonic,' I tells her, 'Don't come no nearer.'

Only she says, 'You got nothing of the sort, Kitty.' Then she sees me trying to wash my knickers and says, 'What you've got's perfectly natural, my girl, and from now on you'll get it every month till you're older than me even.'

Well I just stood there staring at her only she says, 'You stay right there, lovey, and I'll show you what to do about it.' And next thing she's back again with this little towel she folds in an oblong and a clean pair of drawers for me. 'Now you pins the towel inside your knickers like this, before you put them on.'

And I'm still sniffling and I says, 'But what if I mark me dress?'

She says, 'You won't. Here, see this?' and she give me this little apron to wear behind me back to front like, only under me skirt. 'There, you are,' she says. 'Now you'll be right as rain.' I must have looked not sure still, cos she says. 'Cheer up, you ain't going to die. Ethel and Dolly got it at your age, and Mabel too and so will Maisie when her time come.' Then she left.

I stood there for a bit feeling I don't know what. I don't know what it is I got or why, all I know is it ain't plague. Thank goodness.

**31st March, Saturday**

It were Ma's birthday today, the same day as they tell us our house is coming down, along with Reggie's next door and them's the other side. Ma said it weren't a very nice thing but to tell a body on their birthday, specially when the body don't know where it'll be spending the night. Fred and Artie give her a picture of roses they got from a second-hand shop up town and said it come out of their rat money. Ma said it were lovely. Me and Maisie give her samplers we done at school and she said they was lovely too.

I hope we don't have to sleep out in the open tonight with them big piles of rubbish and all them dead rats. I don't know what's worse, live rats scuttling over up in the ceiling or dead ones lying all round me.

The people in Orange want the capital city to be built there. They say they got nice rainfall and even with hot days the nights are cool and good for chests.

**1st April, Sunday**

We slept in Ragged School, on the floor next to the Cooks and other families. Some have gone to other halls or, if there's room, to friends or family that'll have them. It felt strange sleeping in your own school even with all the desks and chairs pushed aside. Only the Salvation Army and City Mission brung in mattresses and blankets and they give us sandwiches and cups of tea tonight. All the churches stayed open with special prayers for plague.

### 2nd April, Monday

Reggie's still not said nothing about his Valentine. I asked him real casual like how's he like cleaning up and he said he's too busy to scratch hisself. Seems to me he's forgotten and all he thinks about now is rubbish. Least that's all he talks about.

He said there's thousands of tons of rubbish every day gets dumped out at sea. I thought he were joking that there couldn't be that much and I told him April Fool's were yesterday. Only he said he weren't and to come and see for meself. So then he took me down the wharves where all the barges was loaded up ready. Garbage, silt, even sewage, he says is piled up on them.

And I said, 'You mean what's straight from the privies?'

And he said yes. He says they're filling in all the open cess-pits and from now on houses'll have to connect up to the sewer.

'What'll that mean?' I said.

He said, for starters, we'll get a toilet that flushes, not a drop closet or night man as comes round each night to change the pail.

I heard Pa tell Ma there's yards he's seen would give

her the horrors. Cess-pits in butcher's yards right next the chopping block and the joints and sausages hanging up all covered in flies. I felt sick when I heard him and didn't feel like any tea only the stew they give us smelt all right and since it come in from outside the Rocks it must be safe.

There's been somebody died of it today, over North Sydney and another in the city. That's two more.

### 3rd April, Tuesday

*The Herald* says there's New South Wales Mounteds been in some fighting yesterday at Karee Siding. There were a thousand British and Colonials with forty-two guns up against three thousand Boers with even more guns and a maxim besides. Reggie says that's some sort of machine gun. In the end but the British lost nineteen dead and a hundred and fifty-nine wounded. I don't know if the Boers lost any.

Ma read out today about this lady doctor as got herself a job with the government. She's been in India and is real good with plague, even though she comes from Tasmania. Her name's Dr Sadie Morie and Ma said isn't that nice, a lady doctor. I think that'd be a nice thing to be if I hadn't already said I were going to be a typist or a telephone lady.

There's a young man died of plague, 24. Not much older than Bertie and yesterday was to have been his wedding day. And when he come down sick and went into quarantine on the 25th of March his fiancée said could she nurse him, only they said no. And now he's dead.

Mr Oliver's been to see more places and says there's maybe a couple in Monaro would make good capital cities. Bombala and Delegate but I've never heard of them.

### 4th April, Wednesday

Queen Victoria's been on a visit to Ireland and they put up nine miles of decorations just for her to drive through from where she come ashore to where she got out of her carriage in the park. There was £10 000 spent on fancy lights as well. Fred says that's an awful lot to spend on lights.

### 5th April, Thursday

Fred's birthday today only we told him he had to wait till Saturday to get his present cos he's getting a present to share with Artie. Just as well his comes first. Artie couldn't have waited.

### 6th April, Friday

You'd hardly know our street any more. I went there today and it looks more like some place in Africa where there's been fighting, not like Sydney. I know they had to pull down houses that you couldn't live in no more and they'll put up new ones instead only they'll be different so the Rocks'll never really look the same again, will it? That's a bit sad really.

Two more today.

There's been no word from Bertie now for ages. I hope he's all right and that he got my letter. Ma used to worry about him all the time, only now she says she's got so much to worry about what with where we'll be living after clean-up and if Pa'll have a job, that she don't have time to worry about Bertie too. He's just got to look after hisself.

Mr Oliver's gone to look at Bombala.

## 7th April, Saturday

It were Artie's birthday today and we give them their present. It's a billycart Pa's been making out back behind the school when they was in bed. He done it from bits he's scrounged on clean-up. Miss Collins let him hide it in a shed out back during the day. Harrington Street's on a bit of a hill, only not real bumpy with bricks and stuff lying round so they'll be safe there. They were that happy when they seen it and couldn't wait to try it out. Pa says they got take turn and turn about dragging it up the top of the street. All the other kids round wanted a go as well, so after a bit they was all taking turns.

## 8th April, Sunday

Tonight Pa brung home some Sunday paper he found, just
to show Ma the adverts in for plague. He says there's
people around who'll try and sell you anything as makes
money. 'Like this: Plague! The Black Death! The Scourge
of the East! Take Dr Morse's Indian Root Pills and avoid
it! There, what'd I tell you?' he says only Ma says there's
nobody's going to start telling her what to take.

Then he finds an advert for PROTECTIVE
ANKLETS and Maisie wants to know what anklets is.

Ma says they're like socks only for round the ankles.
Then Maisie wants to know what they do. Ma says she's
getting worse by the minute with her questions and the
anklet's s'posed to stop the fleas getting up your leg.

Only Pa laughs and says he bets all them people on
the trams are wishing they had a pair ever since Fred and
Artie carted all them fleas up town.

## 9th April, Monday

There's someone from Woolloomooloo got it now. And
there's been lots more rats round. Bondi this time and Ma
says they'd be after the picnic scraps. Fred and Artie been
out again today looking and Ma says they can take them up
Bathurst Street so long as they're stone dead and dumped in
boiling water first. She told Pa it's only got to take one to
run up their leg and they'll soon change their minds.

Fred and Artie wear short pants still, as just cover their

72

knees. They'd get a terrible fright. Reggie's too tall now for short trousers and he wears his pa's cut down a bits.

### 10th April, Tuesday

There's a little boy died of it. Three and a half he was. They took him to North Head and he died before his ma could see him. Now there's another two come down in Waverley.

Moore Park tips's to be covered over with sand and the open sewer that goes from George Street to Blackwattle Bay's being closed in. Wexford Street as runs off Campbell where Mr Ah Han lives has that many rats all through, they've had to send a clean-up gang specially. The whole street and all its houses is to come down. Chinese men come forward and said they'd like to work on clean-up, only they weren't allowed. It don't seem fair when you think it's their houses and they got no other work.

It makes me feel funny when I hear whole streets are coming down. There's streets round here me and other kids used to play in, lanes some of them, real narrow and barely twelve feet wide maybe. Now they're gone. Dead ends good for hiding or playing ball and none of them there now. Nothing's going to look the same any more.

## 11th April, Wednesday

There's a little girl, Emily Shaw, come down with it. Her family took her to Children's Hospital, only they said she had it and they went off to quarantine.

## 13th April, Good Friday

Ma said we was all to go to church this morning, that she'd take us girls and Pa was to take Fred and Artie. She said it's Good Friday and the least we could do was say thank you for us not getting plague. City Mission held prayers and hymns in Ragged School for everyone as wanted them, only Ma said she was going to St Mary's, even if she had to crawl under the barricades to get there. They put a cross up, all draped in purple for Easter. And Pa said there was lots of people at St Andrews, only Artie wouldn't sit still cos the lady in front had a big hat with feathers and he said he couldn't see.

There's been a hundred and four people sick with it so far and thirty-six dead besides.

The paper had adverts in today for fish, it being Good Friday, only they're saying none of it come from Sydney Harbour. It's all from up north round Brisbane Waters where there's no disinfectant killed them off.

## 15th April, Easter Sunday

It's raining and turned real cold all of a sudden and the wind's that strong Pa says it's times like this he's glad he don't have a boat, cos he wouldn't want to be out on the harbour with it blowing a gale like this. At least now he says the rats'll start to disappear. Maybe.

It's still pretty crowded in Ragged School what with the families living there, and sometimes there's fights between us kids, only there's always some ma or pa steps in to stop it on account of nobody can help not having a house no more and having to camp. The food's all right but. Nothing special. North Head were better, but there's bread most days and we get soup or stews at night.

## 16th April, Monday

Freezing cold still. Thought I'd freeze to death last night the hall's that draughtly and we only got a thin blanket each. But me and Maisie snuggled up together and shared both ours to keep warm.

Fred and Artie ain't found theirselves one rat since Saturday.

Pa says there's people down China Town been attacked in the street and stones thrown at them. And one man's gone and killed hisself on account of he'd been beaten up and his business ruined and he had no work and no money. Pa says it's like a war almost the way people are treating them and Mr Ah Duck—that were his name—didn't deserve to be treated that bad. The Chinese got every right to live in the city same as the rest of us.

A letter come from Mabel today from Woodstock up the Blue Mountains wanting to know how we are and do we need anything. Mrs Alexander got her to write, only Ma said she probably just wants to know if we've come down with something nasty for when Mabel visits on her next day off. Pa said that weren't fair but Ma said all she knew was Mrs Alexander took Mabel up the mountains cos she couldn't do without a maid, not cos she were worried about Mabel.

I were surprised to hear Ma talk like that, specially when she's always wanting me to go into service too. Only maybe Ma's starting to think different now? I hope so.

### 17th April, Tuesday

Still cold and no rats about but that don't stop the adverts. There's sales on at all the big shops, because people are nervous going out to shop Pa says. And there's adverts for bicycles so you won't have to go on the trams or buses. You can even buy insurance for plague only it wouldn't have done Cannibal Tom much good.

### 18th April, Wednesday

Today were the coldest day in April for forty-one years the *Herald* said. Doesn't surprise me. My arms is covered in goose bumps and have been all day.

Ma's reading real well now, only it's harder to give her practice what with lots of other people round. Pa still brings the paper home when he can find one, only Ma don't want the other ladies to know she's learning. I told her that were silly that there's some of them can't read neither. I told Miss Collins who said Ma was welcome to come in her office any time. So now Ma takes herself off there whenever she got a spare moment. There's books there too she can read as well and that's more interesting than adverts and bits of paper.

**19th April, Thursday**

There's no word come from England yet on whether they'll let us have a federation. Pa says they're probably more taken with the war and besides federation got nothing to do with them.

The wind died down this morning and finally the sun come out. Now Fred and Artie are hoping all the rats'll come back. They're the only ones in Sydney as does but. Fred says he's saving up to buy for fireworks for Empire Day.

**20th April, Friday**

Today a letter come from Bertie. We were that excited everyone wanted to open it only it were addressed to me on account of I wrote to him first so I got to. I read it out and now everyone's heard it and I'm going to slip it in the pages of my diary to keep it safe.

*Dear Kitty*

*Thanks for your letter which were delivered to me in hospital in Bloemfontein where I come down with typhoid. Our lot's taken over the Parliament House here for a hospital because there's an epidemic on that's pretty bad. Most of us got typhoid drinking river water not knowing it was crook from bodies of men and horses floating further upstream. And there's been a lot died of it but I've been just lucky I guess. The women of the town pitched in to help the army nurses take care of us and now me and my mates are mostly on the mend.*

*We were almost done for when we rode in. I'd had nothing to eat for thirty hours except a biscuit and half a corn cob. But if we were plum tuckered out, the horses were worse off, half-starved poor things and ready to drop most of them. We lost two thousand on the ride in. Just had to leave them on one side and hope we could maybe walk the rest of the way, if we couldn't get another horse. We can usually pick up a remount, a horse that's lost its trooper, if we're lucky. Otherwise, it's Shanks' pony.*

*Most of the way you could hear the sound of shots every time a trooper put his horse down rather than make him go on. And now we're here, there's mounds of dead horses piled up, three hundred in some places and twelve hundred others sick besides.*

*Bloemfontein's a town of probably five thousand people only for now there's maybe 50 000 to 60 000 troopers as well, so it's pretty crowded. The townspeople weren't at all keen to see Australians. Almost hostile some of them, saying we shouldn't have come. We're*

*farmers like them and how come we joined the British?*
*Threw me back a bit I can tell you. All I know is, I come*
*over for a bit of adventure and so far, I've not seen much*
*of that. Just a lot of dead horses and sick men, those that*
*aren't wounded or killed outright. Most of what I've*
*seen's been on a pretty empty stomach at times. Seems to*
*me there's more troopers dying of sickness in this war*
*than there are of bullets.*

*Anyway, I hope all's well with you at home*
*love to all from your gloomy*

*Bertie.*

And Ma said, 'There, what did I tell you? The army's not
looking after him.'

Pa said, 'No, that's because it's the army.'

### 21st April, Saturday

There's two more cases in Paddo and Summer Hill but the
good news is clean-up gangs have finished round here and
the barricades are down in Kent and Druitt Streets.
There's some down in Liverpool Street and part of Sussex.
Now the gangs have moved on. The men that come from
outside will stay up town from now on, them and the
cooks that feed them.

There's sixty-two people still in quarantine not
counting contacts and a hundred and thirty-four rats was
burnt in Bathurst Street yesterday only the paper says the
old furnace is nearly worn out now and they'll have to get
a new one.

Now the barricades are down the schools'll be going back. Pa says some people will still keep their kids away till there's no more bubonic at all. That could take months. And there's kids roaming the streets whose pa or ma's maybe died of it and Miss Collins got to try and get them to move in. She says she'll take a class down one end for older kids and Miss Nunn can teach the littlies up the other. Ma and the other ladies just got to do their sewing quiet, not chattering round the sides. Ma gets on real well with Miss Collins now and that don't do me no harm, specially if she talks Ma out of sending me off to service.

**23th April, Monday**

George come round to see Pa today. He said he were that sick of coffins and dead people he just had to get away for a bit. So his boss said he could have the rest of the week off just so long as he's back again Monday. Pa told him he looked tired and he ought to get away down the coast, maybe do some fishing. Only George said all he wants to do is see Lily and try to talk her round. It's only because she's scared she won't see him so he got to make her understand he's had his needle and has had all this time and he's ever so careful round bodies. Besides somebody has to bury them. They can't just leave them lying out on top can they?

## 24th April, Tuesday

It's still not gone. There's more come down with it.

I hope Bertie's all right now and got over the typhoid.

## 25th April, Wednesday

I know what federation means only I heard Pa saying
England thinks we should keep the right of appeal.
'What's that?' I said and it seems the Queen's got this
council of three hundred men to advise her. It's a bit like
a court you take cases to and I said, 'What we need a
court for when we got our own?' And Pa says it's just
they want us to stay part of the Empire, not break away
proper. I'm not sure I know what he means only I don't
s'pose it matters so long as we have our own federation.

## 27th April, Friday

Ma wrote her first letter today to Mabel. Miss Collins and I
helped a bit but Ma did most of it by herself in quite nice
writing too. She wanted to show Mabel she could do it.
She's real proud of herself too. Ma come from a big family
and went into service because there was always little ones
as had to be fed so everybody pitched in. It weren't
something she liked, just something as had to be done.

But with Mabel it were different. All she ever wanted to

do when she was little was play with her dolly, curl its hair and dress it up. Soon as she got bigger, all she ever wanted was to be lady's maid. All I hope is that Mrs Alexander treats her well. Some of these la-di-da ladies can be right nags I can tell you, only Mabel don't seem unhappy.

### 28th April, Saturday

Pa and Ma been married twenty-five years today and Ma said she's hardly had time to sit down all that time. She's been that busy and she must look a fright. Only Pa told her she didn't look a day older than when he married her.

Ma give him a smile and said, 'Oh get away with you.' But I could see she were pleased just the same.

### 29th April, Sunday

That thing happened to me again this month, only this time I weren't scared and didn't need to tell Ma.

### 30th April, Monday

The Show's been on over Easter. Only Ma said she couldn't afford to take us. Maisie and Artie wanted to look at the animals and Fred wanted to see if they had any motor cars displayed. I didn't say nothing only I wanted to see the new typewriters come all the way from America. I don't have the money to buy one but I'd still like to see them.

**1st May, Tuesday**

No word about the essay competition. I thought they must have decided and nobody had bothered to say who'd won it. Only this morning Pa said he'd read where they made the date for closing later on account of the plague and everything being topsy-turvy like. Still that were the start of April so they should know by now.

There's two more died of it today.

**2nd May, Wednesday**

I've been doing lots of skipping lately and Ma says I'm starting to look more like a young lady than a harum scarum. And she says if she had the money she'd buy me a real pretty dress for my birthday and maybe some proper stays to go under it so I'd be all nipped in at the waist like. Only she don't have money to spare for either just now so I just got to be happy with what God give me. I wouldn't mind seeing meself in a mirror but, to see if she's right and I do have a waist now.

## 3rd May, Thursday

I went to get my skipping rope after school to try out this
new rhyme I heard.

*Mabel, Mabel,*
*Set the table,*
*Don't forget the vinegar, salt, pepper.*

Only there were no sign of it and when I asked Ma she
said she hadn't seen it neither. So then I went outside and
found that Fred and Artie had tied it to the front of their
billycart rope so's to make it longer. Talk about cheek!
Only they said please could they have it for a bit longer
still and I had to say yes all right but only for a lend mind
and soon as they'd finished hauling it up they got to give
it back. Now I'll have to do my skipping after tea tonight.

## 4th May, Friday

Ma reads all the adverts by herself now and hardly ever
has to ask for help. She says Anthony Hordern's got tailor-
made coats and skirt costumes in black and navy. She
looked a bit sad when she said it like she wished she could
have something smart like that for best, instead of her old
dark dress and jacket. But I said never mind, she was sure
to one day. Then we looked at each other and laughed and
both of us said, 'When your ship come in!' Then I give
her a bit of a hug and she said it means a lot to her being
able to read now and she's real glad I'd showed her and I
said, 'That's all right Ma,' and give her a kiss.

## 5th May, Saturday

It were Reggie's birthday today. He's turned 14 already
and his ma and pa give him a new shirt and a new pair of
trousers for his own, not his pa's cut downs.

## 6th May, Sunday

Ma says maybe if she don't get any more people that
wants washing done after this is all over she should
maybe find something else to do that'll bring in a bit of
money still. Besides she's quite happy to give away all
that standing and scrubbing. So I said what about getting
a sewing machine then she could sit down and maybe
make things for us and her and other people p'raps. She
said it were a good idea, only she weren't sure how much
a treadle machine would cost. So now we're watching the
adverts to see if there's one going cheap.

## 7th May, Monday

There's more businesses up for sale now. Pages and pages
of adverts. You can get a grocery's, butcher's or
confectioner's shop even. Maisie wanted to know what a
confectioner's was and Fred said lollies and ice-creams,
only before Maisie could ask her Ma said that were the
last thing she needed.

'What about a poultry farm then, Ma,' I said. 'Here's five acres at Parramatta and you and chooks get on well together.'

Ma grinned and said, 'Here, none of your lip.'

## 9th May, Wednesday

Ethel and Dolly come to see us today and Ethel's got this funny smile on her face and tells Ma she's stepping out with a young man from her factory. They only knew each other to nod to before and I thought that don't surprise me. Her factory's that noisy all you could do is nod.

Anyway, seems she met up with him waiting in line for inoculations and since then they've been on picnics to Victoria Park. Only Ma said, 'You mean to tell me, my girl, you been out on a picnic with a man, and on your own?' But Ethel says it weren't on her own, Dolly come too. Then Dolly chipped in and said Ethel's young man weren't much of a looker, but he was ever so nice to Ethel and thinks she's got lovely hair. Ethel's on the fair side, only not as fair as Maisie and Artie. Dolly and Mabel got dark hair like George.

Anyway, Ethel told Dolly to hush up, that Albert (that's his name) has promised to take her ice-skating, soon as the factory starts again and he's got a bit of money to his name. I were that envious when I heard. Nobody's ever asked me to go ice-skating only when I said so later to Ma she said even if they did I wouldn't be going. I'm far too young to be stepping out with anybody. Worst luck.

## 10th May, Thursday

There's been five more cases today, from all over and one
in China Town, Mr Ah How. Now the Council's saying
they want to build a morgue for people that dies of it in
the city and they want to put it at Dawes Point or Millers
but Pa says there's no way he wants a morgue right on his
back doorstep.

   He's had to give Ethel and Dolly some money to help
pay their rent on account of they're behind. But their
factories went back this week so they should have money
in time for next week's.

## 11th May, Friday

There were a Chinese man over in Botany got plague and
his council demanded to see every Chinese house around.
Not all the houses, just Chinese ones, which don't seem
fair. Afterwards they said the houses were really clean
inside, only awful outside and no human beings should
have to live in them. They ain't got proper drains even
and the council says they should all be pulled down.

   Ma shook her head when she heard. She says it's not
right people having to live like that let alone being treated
bad for it. Mr Ah Han told her if a family got nowhere to
live they just puts a packing case in someone's backyard for
them till they find somewhere. And Ma told him there were
no way he could fit a packing case that big in our backyard.

   Mr Ah Han just grinned and said, 'Plenty room, Missy.'

## 12th May, Sunday

I keep thinking of Mr Ah Han and his horse and how's he going to feed him if he got no work. So this morning I went to Mass and said a prayer for him and his horse and then I said one for Bertie and all the troopers' horses as well.

## 14th May, Monday

I've not seen as much of Reggie since St Joseph's went back. Only when everyone has tea of a night. Today but he asked me straight out if maybe I'd found a note left in our letter-slit a while back and I said, 'Yes, there were letters come through. Only Pa took them.'

Reggie went a bit red and said but maybe there were one addressed to me.

I give nothing away only just frowned a bit as if I were trying to remember and said, 'Oh yes Pa did give me one.'

Reggie said, 'Were it a poem like?'

I said, 'Yes I think so. Round Valentine's. Oh dear, were that from you Reggie?' Then I give him a smile so he know I'm teasing.

## 16th May, Saturday

There's been Mounted Rifles in the thick of fighting lately. That'll be Bertie's lot. At Zand River and

Kroonstad and the general in charge has sent a cable to Mr Lyne saying what fine soldiers they are and Pa says it don't surprise him one bit, he always knew Bertie and them would do us proud. There's more troopers gone since Bertie's lot and there's talk of more still. Bertie said in a letter to Pa some Boer families got maybe a father and sons fighting and it's sad if you see them all killed. Only the British army got the Empire behind it so they can always get more troopers.

**18 May, Friday**

Mafeking's been saved! Yesterday. It took fifteen hundred troopers to do it. That's the last of the towns under siege. This time it were two hundred and seventeen days. Imagine being cooped up that long! And there's huge crowds gathered in London, almost like New Year's Eve going mad with excitement. Everybody cheering and yelling and singing and shaking hands with perfect strangers, they're that happy. And come night time all these fireworks were set off.

There were people all over Sydney started celebrating soon as they heard too. Down the wharves and up in the Post Office and all over the city. And you could hear church bells ringing out. And down on the *Sabraon*, the boys' training ship, the captain sent all the boys up the rigging to give three cheers for Mafeking!

The colonel in charge was Baden-Powell. Now they're saying he's a hero for keeping them alive. Only when Ma heard she looked real suspicious and 'Yeah, but how?'

I said, 'What d'you mean?'

She said, 'Was there fair rations?' Ma's always fair
when it come to dividing up. Even if she's only had bread
and dripping and a cup of tea, we all get what's fair
allowing for little people like Maisie and big like Pa. 'I'll
bet that colonel give the black people less so's he could
give the white people more.' I don't know if Ma's right
but it don't sound fair if she is.

### 19th  May, Saturday

There's to be a holiday Wednesday, special, to celebrate
Mafeking. And there'll be bands playing in Hyde Park
and a 21-gun salute from Dawes Point and lots of
buildings lit up that night.

There's a British India steam ship coming with 20 000
more doses of Haffkine's that goes in the needles they
give you. Maybe that'll help stop it.

### 20th May, Sunday

Today when I went looking for my skipping rope I find
Maisie's 'borrowed' it this time. She and Elsie and Jess got
it tied to a basket they're dangling over a railing and
hauling it up and down playing messages. They put notes
in it and little surprises for each other and give their dollies
rides. I had to tell them they could have it for a while only
they have to give it back soon as they've finished.

## 23rd May, Wednesday

It poured buckets today. Started early this morning and didn't let up once, so there were no bands and no guns firing and no buildings lit up tonight. And there won't be troops parading tomorrow neither for the Queen's birthday on account of the ground's too wet for horses. I bet that means it's too wet for fireworks too.

And as if that's not bad enough tomorrow's my birthday when I turn 13 and Ma says I'm to leave Ragged School. She's not said anything about me going into service lately only I know she sees all the adverts for girls wanted now. I expect she's already got something in mind for me. I won't be able to sleep a wink tonight for worry.

## 24th May, Thursday

This morning I woke up hoping Ma would forget it were my birthday but no hope of that. It's Empire Day so it's always a holiday and she can't forget. So when she called me over this morning I felt sure she'd say something, only instead she give me this bit of lace she's saved and said she's going to make me a new chimmy and drawers for best. Then she says, 'And I want to talk to you tonight.' So all day I were moping round till Pa said I'd have to cheer up or I'd set him off crying and if my bottom lip stuck out any more I'd most probably trip over it.

Fred and Artie give me some double bungers, only they kept out of my way cos they could see I were in a bad mood. Maisie give me this picture of a cat she's done and wants to know what's wrong, don't I like it?

I tried not to think about it but and think about Empire Day with all the ships on the harbour decked out in flags and Dawes Battery's gun salute for Her Majesty and HMS *Royal Arthur* done up in lights tonight from stem to stern looking real pretty. But now and then it were hard not to. It's late now and she's still not said nothing, so maybe she has forgotten after all?

## 25th May, Friday

I were wrong. Ma hadn't forgotten. Soon as Maisie and Fred and Artie were settled down, she comes and sits beside me and starts off saying, 'Kitty.' I always get nervous when she starts off Kitty. I think I'm in trouble. 'You're 13 now,' she says.

I say, 'Yes Ma, only please don't make me go into service. I'm not like Mabel. I'd hate it I know and if you let me stay on just a bit longer at school I'll make it up to you somehow, I promise, as soon as I get a job typewriting or with telephones and can pay you back.'

Then guess what? Ma just smiles and says what a silly I am and she's decided I can stay on after all till the end of the year. That's if Miss Collins'll have me. She's ever so grateful I've taught her to read and besides Miss Collins has been talking to her, seeing as how there were no school while clean-up were on and I've missed a bit. I can hardly believe it and throw my arms round her, only she says we'll see how things are next year when I turn

14, what money's coming in, and whether Pa's got work. So for me it turned out to be my best birthday ever.

## 26th May, Saturday

Another person's come down with bubonic yesterday and one dead besides just when we thought it had maybe gone away.

There's been 68 076 rats killed since the 2nd of March! Imagine a pile that big. You'd need an incinerator big as the GPO almost to burn them. I saw Fred trying to work out how much money that'd earn him. And there's been a rat found at Government House and Ma said, 'Well, I never!' when she heard. Only Pa said it didn't have plague. They sent it off for checking and word come back it died normal.

There were horse races held at Randwick today and I asked Pa how come they let horses run when it's muddy only they won't let troopers' horses parade? And he said some horses like it muddy for running and it don't matter if they get splashed, only troopers horses got to look nice on parade not covered in mud, that's all.

All the big buildings in the city were lit up tonight and we got fireworks for Empire Day and Mafeking combined. Twice as many. Pa got us strings and strings of Tom Thumbs and Catherine Wheels, and Fred, Artie and Reggie had lots of double bungers they've been saving up for and rockets and jumping jacks besides. Reggie let a jumping jack off too near Mr Higgs and it shot straight up his trouser leg and he were hopping about yelling out

who done that? and a lot of other things besides he
shouldn't, only it must have hurt a lot. Reggie and Fred
didn't say nothing on account of Mr Higgs didn't know
which of them did it.

Only one new case today.


**28th May, Monday**


Today Miss Collins give me a letter addressed to me that
come to Ragged School after being all round the Rocks
by the look of it. Since we got no house we got no letter-
slit so the postman just has to find us. It were from the
'O.K'. Jam factory to say I shared first prize in the essay
competition with some kid as lives over in Darlinghurst.
The letter said there were lots of girls entered, only not
many boys, so they're not giving a boys' first prize, just a
second and third. That means the other girl and me can
choose between a Morocco leather lady's dressing case or
Morocco leather writing desk. Pa and Ma were that proud
of me and Ma said to take the dressing case. That's what
she always wanted, only Pa said he thought I should go
for the writing desk. They was getting that excited, the
pair of them, I had to tell them to shush, it were my prize
and I'd decide.

Then I looked at the letter and saw it were posted
the 10th of May so I told them maybe it were too late
for any prize.

Pa said, 'We'll see about that!' I love it when Pa says
that like nobody's going to stop his kids from having
things done fair. Only it were after 5 o'clock then and too

late to ring them at the factory. He said we would first thing in the morning.

### 29th May, Tuesday

Pa and me went up to Millers Point post office—that's opposite Lord Nelson Hotel—and rung Peacock's factory from there. Pa spoke to the manager, who was very glad to hear from us on account of he didn't know where to find me. Then he asked to speak to me and said he were very sorry but the other girl had come in and chosen the lady's dressing case.

I said, 'That don't matter, sir. I were going to ask for the writing case anyway.' And the manager sounded real pleased and said any time I cared to call at the factory office my prize'd be waiting.

Pa had to go to work on clean-up that day so after school this afternoon Ma had Mrs Cook mind Maisie and Ma and I got ourselves smartened up and went up town on the electric tram. They only been running since last December so this were our first trip. And we went as far as Parramatta Road and walked to the factory from there.

The manager was ever so nice and shook hands with us both and give us a cup of tea and a biscuit. Then he said my essay were very well thought out and most interesting. I could see Ma beaming all the time. He said the other girl wrote her favourite occupation were riding her new pony. Ma give me a look from behind the manager's back like she weren't the least surprised.

Then he give me the writing case and we come back

down town on the tram. I showed Miss Collins my case and she said it were beautiful and all the kids crowded round to see. Even Reggie. I think he's a bit sorry now he didn't go in the competition.

When you open it up there's paper and ink bottle and blotter roll and a real nice pen. And the leather's smooth and dark shiny red. Then when you go to write something you put the lid down and it's like a little desk almost. The first thing I'm going to do is write a letter to Bertie to tell him about it.

England says we can have federation and Pa says the gold miners in Western Australia have said they want to vote on it so now all of Western Australia will have to vote again.

*The Herald* says the army's only twenty miles from Johannesburg where all the Boer gold mines are.

### 30th May, Wednesday

Seems like all the townspeople cheered as the troopers marched into Johannesburg. Pa says that's because lots of them aren't Boers but British moved there for the gold mining.

President Kruger still says he won't give in but, and Lord Roberts won't get as far as Pretoria, only Pretoria's starting to panic on account of that's the capital city and the British army's getting awfully close now.

There's new notices gone up. One on the wall outside the grocer's.

BOUNTY
6d A HEAD!

Ma says that's outrageous to pay that much for a dead rat. Even Pa says it'd buy him two beers and maybe now he should start collecting rats instead of doing clean-up. Only Fred and Artie's eyes lit up like candles when they heard. I think they're planning maybe they can make hundreds of pounds now. Only the notices say the rats got to be taken in cans with lids on and in disinfectant and taken out again with tongs. So Fred's worked it all out and says he can't afford cans with lids and disinfectant and tongs on top of their tram fares. So he says him and Artie just have to give up the rat business from now on.

**1st June, Friday**

The harbour's been closed. There's no one allowed to go fishing or bathing in it while all that carbolic's still in the water and all them dead fish floating about on top. Pa says there's no way you'd get him eating fish now even if he caught it hisself. He used to take Fred and Artie down the wharf pier before all this happened and they'd sit there hoping to catch us our tea of a night.

My hair's real long now. I keep it tied back from my face and now I'm starting to put it up. Pa says I look quite the young lady when it's all done up neat.

There's going to be a new railway station at Devonshire Street called Central Station. It'll be closer in to the city than Redfern and underneath the city they're going to make tunnels and have railway lines running through them right up as far as St James Road. Pa says that means a lot more people'll be able to come into the city by train. Only I can't see how. If there are buildings already there and they dig tunnels underneath them, won't the buildings fall in?

**3rd June, Sunday**

Ma give me my new unmentionables this morning. The ones she put the lace on and I'm wearing them to Mass today. No one will know what I'm wearing except me. Certainly not Reggie Cook.

**4th June, Monday**

Lord Roberts has ridden into Pretoria at the head of all his troops, so Mr Kruger was wrong. Winston Churchill, who writes for the *Morning Post* in England, rode in in the middle of the night on a bicycle while the Boers were still there! Then he turned round and rode straight back out again with the Governor of the city to where his lordship was waiting. Ma said that were a daft thing to do. A New South Mounted got to take in Lord Roberts' message of Surrender Or Else.

Then all the newspaper writers like Banjo Paterson went in and had the Boer flag taken down and the Union Jack run up in its place and the band ready to play 'God Save the Queen' when his lordship got the keys to the town. Then all the troopers cheered and some of them took photos.

### 5th June, Tuesday

Whenever Ma's busy I got to play with Maisie, keep her out of Ma's way. She's always wanting to brush my hair only sometimes she gets the brush tangled and I got to undo it. After that she wants me put her hair up so's she can pretend she's 'growed up'.

### 6th June, Wednesday

I sometimes think how lucky Elsie and Jess were not getting plague when their pa did. And how lucky Maisie and Eddy have been as well. There's a little girl, Lilian Stephens, come down with it now, and a man died over in quarantine. Just shows you there's some not been so lucky.

Clean-up gangs started over in Manly today and one house they pulled down had thirty rats under the floorboards all dead and rotting. The stink were that bad the men had to keep rushing out and gulping fresh air before going back in.

**7th June, Thursday**

Dr Ashburton Thompson's the man in charge of getting rid of plague. He says slums in Sydney are some of the worst he's ever seen, even worse than London, where he comes from. Only Ma said did he have to say that in the paper where everyone reads it. It's embarrassing enough for them that has to live in them.

**8th June, Friday**

Really big storm yesterday. Rough seas and winds of 60 mile an hour and cold. Still cold today too. It's times like this I wish we were back in our old bedroom, not in a draughty school hall. At least there with six of us it were warmer.

Maisie had a nightmare last night and woke up crying.

I said, 'What's wrong, Maisie?'

She says, 'Where will we live now? We don't have a house no more. Will we ever have a house again, Kitty?'

So I give her a cuddle and tell her not to worry, that Pa will fix everything up. And once all the clean-ups

done they'll start building houses. She seemed to settle
down after that, only then I lay awake wondering. With
all this talk of houses being built, is Pa going to have the
money for one?

**9th June, Saturday**

I asked him this morning and he said, not to worry my
pretty head about it. So I hope it's all right.

There were a big meeting in Sydney this week. It
seems lots of people want the Premier to get a bill passed
to give women the vote. They say if Mr Lyne gets one
passed soon, we could have it in time for federation
voting. I asked Ma what she thought and she said of
course women should be able to vote. They can't make
any more of a mess of things than men.

There's been over a thousand babies born in May and
that's far more than the number of people who've died.
Ma says it's nice somehow to think of little babies
making up for all those poor people that got sick and died
of plague.

**10th June, Sunday**

Dolly come over this arvo and said she had something
she wanted to talk about. Only it's hard with other
families round all the time. So Ma said why don't we go
for a walk and we all went up Observatory Hill. I had to

play with Maisie and keep her out of their way and the boys ran about by themselves. Only it turns out Dolly says she's tired of working in the factory and wants to do something else. And Pa said what for instance when she got no training. Then Dolly says she'd like to go nursing. Ma and Pa seem stunned only they don't say she's not to or anything. Pa just says she should maybe write to the matron at Sydney Hospital and see what she has to say. I told Dolly I thought it were a wonderful idea and I'm real proud of her.

### 11th June, Monday

I'm spending more time playing with Maisie these days on account of Ma still don't like her wandering round the Rocks on her own. There's houses going up and she could get in the way. So I showed her how to make dollies' clothes out of scraps Ma give us. Now Topsy's got a new dress that's ever so smart and she don't look so bad no more.

### 12th June, Tuesday

It's Ethel's birthday today. Ma said when she had Ethel she were that pleased she were a girl. She was beginning to think maybe all she'd ever have was boys.

## 14th June, Thursday

There's been two more cases today and the paper says war's broken out in China now. Pa says we won't be sending troopers to this one.

## 15th June, Friday

There's another two more people got it today so it's not gone, not by a long chalk.

## 16th June, Saturday

Mr Oliver's been to Braidwood now and looked at that for a capital city. I wonder where they'll end up putting it and what they'll call it after all that.

## 17th June, Sunday

We've met Ethel's young man. Very polite to Ma he was and seems very fond of Ethel. Not much to say for himself but, as Pa says, he would have had a hard time getting a word in what with Ma and Ethel, Maisie and me all talking at once.

### 19th June, Tuesday

Bertie's pay's been coming in regular and Ma's saving what she can. He did say he wanted to help out so she's putting aside for us too. There's bound to be things she needs for the new house when it's built. No sign of it starting even yet.

### 22nd June, Friday

The House of Commons in England has said we can have a federation. Pa says it took them long enough but. And there'll be celebrations for a whole week all over the country when we get it. It'll be like being in a new country almost and just in time for starting off the 20th Century.

### 26th June, Tuesday

Three new cases today. I've lost count how many that is so far.

### 27th June, Wednesday

I've had another one of them things I got back in March when Ma catched me out in the wash house. That's three times now. I don't know what you call it still. Ma didn't say and I don't like to ask.

28th June, Thursday

No one sick today. I wonder what'll happen to all those people that's buried at North Head. It's not like an ordinary cemetery where you can go any time and put flowers on the graves. No one'll be able to go there just for that. So people will have nowhere to visit and feel close.

**29th June, Friday**

Two more deaths for the cemetery at North Sydney.

Reggie told Fred and Artie there's going to be a new bridge over to Pyrmont. It'll go from the bottom of Market Street across Darling Harbour. Reggie wants to build bridges. Only you have to be an engineer first. He says this bridge will swing round in the middle to open up and let ships through. Fred and Artie can't wait to see it working, only Reggie says it'll take them two whole years to build.

## 30th June, Saturday

Ethel's been made an inspector at her factory. Instead of just putting in laces in boots and packing them, now she has to make sure each pair's perfect with no stitching coming undone or nails sticking up inside that could hurt someone. It means extra money for her each week. That's good too.

## 1st July, Sunday

No one's said anything at Ragged School about me being 13 now and should have left. I'm sure Miss Collins don't mind me there and next year so long as Pa's got work I'll go on somewhere else and stay till I turn 15 and done me Junior.

## 2nd July, Monday

It's not as crowded now with other schools back and some families gone already. There's a few houses finished and more going up. Lessons go on same as usual but, and Ma's taken to sitting on one side when we do spelling and I can tell she's practising in her head to get it right.

### 3rd July, Tuesday

There's going to be memorials all round Sydney for troopers that's died in the war. There's one going up for Lieutenant Grieve out at Watson's Bay and a plaque for Corporal Kilpatrick at Leichhardt Public. And Lieutenant Harriott's to have one at St Thomas North Sydney inside the church and maybe the gates as well. I think it's nice to have something to remember them.

### 5th July, Thursday

The House of Lords has passed the bill for Federation Pa says, and our first Governor-General might be Lord Hopetoun. He's been Governor of Victoria already so he should know what to do.

Mr Oliver's been and looked at Bathurst now.

### 6th July, Friday

We've had horrid weather. Pouring rain and cold and blowing a gale again. There's huge waves hit Manly too, and trees are pulled up all over Sydney, as well as telegraph lines down. No one can send a telegram in or out of the city, and up the Blue Mountains there's been snow. Some places even got floods. Why can't it just be pleasant instead of too hot and sticky or freezing cold to chill your bones?

## 8th July, Sunday

Mr Kruger's told Lord Roberts the Boers will go on fighting even if there's only 500 of them left and that could take for ages. There's more troopers gone over from Australia since Bertie left.

A whole week's gone by without one person getting plague.

## 9th July, Monday

The Queen's signed the bit of paper to say we can have Federation. Queen Victoria's my favourite queen on account of she's got freckles too. At least that's what Ma said when I told her I hated mine. But I sometimes wonder how Ma knew?

## 10th July, Tuesday

Mabel come to see us today. It seems Mr and Mrs Alexander come back to the city last weekend to get away from the snow and cold and they give Mabel the day off. She says she were thrilled to get Ma's letter, only it made her feel homesick.

'Don't they treat you right?' said Ma starting to bristle. Mabel says it weren't that, it's just that they're not her real family and since she's on her own mostly she gets lonely.

Mrs Alexander's always going out to parties and dinners and concerts and no sooner has Mabel got her dressed ready than she's left by herself for hours, sewing tiny tears in things or missing buttons or maybe sorting washing and ironing. She don't see no one, only downstairs maids maybe when she has her meals, or the housekeeper if she has to. So Ma give her a bit of a hug and I felt mean we'd said them things about all she her ever wanted were lady's maid.

No cases for eight days now. Maybe it's gone at last?

## 12th July, Thursday

Artie wants to know where the Governor-General's going to live? He could stay in Government House for a while as a visitor, only that's the Governor's house so he can't stay there for long. So they're going to have to find somewhere else for him to live.

## 13th July, Friday

Pa says other countries have heard we're going to be a Federation and France has put a message in one of their papers saying, 'A great nation is thus born.' That were good of them.

Ma and I played a trick on Pa tonight. We've been waiting to let it slip that Ma can read, so no sooner had he finished with the paper tonight than Ma picks it up real casual like and starts reading out loud.

'It says here the chief of the tribe of Kalenza, Chilimonzie, has got 56 wives and 118 children and he's very rich.'

Pa said, 'He'd need to be with that many kids to look after. Nine's bad enough.' Then he frowned and said, 'Hey! How come you read that?'

Ma said, 'Because I can read now, that's why. And I can write. Kitty's been teaching me,' and she put her arm round me.

'Well I never,' said Pa shaking his head like he could hardly believe it. 'I'm real proud of you, Ma,' he said and give her a kiss on the cheek to prove it.

Ma beamed. 'Maybe you should start bringing home two *Heralds* from now on Pa, one for each of us,' she said.

### 14th July, Saturday

Another letter come from Bertie today. It must have been in written in June on account of it was after some battle they was in back then and the mail takes a month to come from South Africa.

*Dear Kitty,*

*I'm over the typhoid, only I make extra sure of any water now before filling my water bottle when we come to a river. The food's terrible still and it's a wonder the army don't kill us all off that way. There's times I long for a plate of Ma's scones and I've even dreamt of her rabbit stew, only to wake up and find there's only bully beef and biscuits for breakfast same as usual. I don't think the British realised just how big this country is and how long it would take supply wagons to get through to us what with oxen and mules pulling them.*

*We've just come through some heavy fighting at Diamond Hill. There were Australians on the left of the column as we rode in this valley and not much firing at first. Only soon as we come out the other side, the Boers start firing in earnest. Their big guns were all on the hills around us. Our lot were off their horses quick smart and climbing up this hill to fire back. Only it wasn't nearly as high as the Boers' and by this time some of their snipers were taking aim from lower down. All the time their shells were pounding us and the horses were dropping dead— some in agony we didn't have time to go back and shoot. We couldn't get away ourselves.*

*Then some of us charged the Boojers hoping to capture their guns, but the firing was so heavy we were forced back. It went on till nightfall without let up. Then our big guns were brought up. Only by then some of the Boers had got clean away and the rest were still firing for all their worth. So we charged again. This time New Souths, West Australians and 6th Mounteds, riding across this open ground so far out in front the British thought we were Boers escaping and started firing at us from both sides. It's a miracle we weren't shot by our own side.*

*Anyway, soon as we reached the Boers' hill, we dismounted and started climbing. Terribly steep it was, but the rocks gave some shelter from the firing up top, only the closer we got the more the bullets poured down. Then next thing there's these two officers yelling at us to move forward. Standing up, no cover at all. We couldn't believe it. Suddenly Lieutenant Harriott cops a bullet in his thigh that shatters it. The other, Drage, gets it in the leg and head and dies almost straight away. Harriott was in terrible pain but all we could do was leave him with a bit of shelter round till we could get him back down to hospital. He died next day on the operating table. Lieutenant Drage and he were really good officers, popular with the blokes, so we all feel down about it. Harriott in particular was good enough to be asked by Lord Roberts to join his personal staff. Such a waste.*

*Glad to hear none of you came down with plague. Sorry about the house. Still, if it means you get something better, that's not too bad.*

*Love to all the family, from your trooper*
*Bertie.*

### 15th July, Sunday

Mabel's birthday today and she got given the day off. Ma met up with her at St Mary's and bring her back here. Then in the arvo Dolly come over with a big tin of jam and Ma and some of the other ladies made scones for everyone. Then just as Mabel were leaving Ma slipped her five shillings to spend for herself.

I showed Bertie's letter to Reggie. I didn't think Bertie would mind since Reggie's always wanting to know where Bertie is now and if he's been in any fighting. Boys are always interested in guns. Fred and Artie are the same.

## 16th July, Monday

The government wants to take back all the land round Dawes and Millers Point. They say it's to make it easier getting from Darling Harbour to the city. Only it means more houses coming down as if enough haven't come down already. And streets'll be moved.

Artie wanted to know how come they can move a whole street. I said if houses come down both sides there's no street left so you can move it anywhere. The government says it'll look much better after. Newer too, only Ma says we liked some of the funny old houses, even if they was dirty and run-down. Now it feels like we're moving somewhere only staying put at the same time.

Maisie's other tooth come through this week. Nice and straight and Ma says that's a blessing. Only now she got a lower one loose.

## 17th July, Tuesday

Dolly's heard back from the matron at Sydney Hospital and she has to go and see her sometime next month.

## 18th July, Wednesday

It's official now, Pa says. Lord Hopetoun is going to be the Governor-General. He's sailing from London soon and will arrive in Sydney in December. Only the Premier of South Australia wants to start the Commonwealth early on the 1st of October, even if Lord Hopetoun isn't here. But you can't have a Federation without a Governor-General, can you? Lady Hopetoun's coming and the children, except the eldest son Lord Hope. I'll bet he got teased at school with a name like that. He's staying in England for a year. Then he'll come out with their carriages and all their horses. I wonder how many he's got but?

Mr Oliver has two more places to look at then he has to write a report to give to the Premier. It must be hard finding somewhere in New South Wales that's big enough and still 100 miles from Sydney. Members of parliament would like it closer, only it's got to be 100 miles.

### 19th July, Thursday

There's been no one come down with it today. That's good.

Somebody's written a letter to the *Herald* saying we should think up a good name for the capital city. Something short and easy to say only dignified. Like Hopetoun. But Pa says what happens when Lord Hopetoun's gone and nobody can remember why they called it that. Besides Hopetoun sounds real English to me.

No plague today either.

Taylor's jam factory, that's rival to Dolly's, have an advert in today. They're giving away free pictures of all the army top brass with every pot of jam. You can have Lord Roberts and Lord Kitchener and Colonel Baden-Powell up on your wall. Only Ma said what would she want them for? She can find plenty of things to upset her without having them staring down at her. Besides, she said it wouldn't be fair to Dolly, specially after I won her factory's competition and she can always get jam for us a bit cheaper.

**21st July, Saturday**

I couldn't believe it today. Reggie Cook said he were thinking of maybe joining up.

I said, 'What for?'

He said, 'To fight the Boojers of course.'

But I told him he were too young. Only he says buglers and drummers go at 14 and he could easy put his age up again, like clean-up, because he's tall.

So I said, 'Reggie Cook, I've never heard nothing so silly in all my life. Besides I got enough to worry about with Bertie over there without having to worry about you too.' Then he give me this funny little smile only it seemed to shut him up.

Maisie's worried and worried that tooth of hers. She

115

keeps pushing it forwards and back. Now she says it's sore. And Ma says she's not surprised, to leave it alone. I can remember having a tooth like that flapping in me mouth and driving me mad so I wiggled it till it finally come out.

### 22nd July, Sunday

It's been a week now since the last person come down with plague and nobody's died of it since the 29th of June.

We've had so much rain lately they can't do any clean-up. They got as far as the bit between Abercrombie Street and Newtown Road. Only there's been a lot of rats found out along Burwood Road, so they're not done there yet.

The paper says 63 464 rats been killed since March.

### 24th July, Tuesday

An Australian's won the Victoria Cross. It's our first. He's Captain Neville Howse and Pa says he's a doctor as well. This trumpeter fell off his horse wounded. Captain Howse galloped over to get him. All the time the Boers kept on firing at them. Captain Howse's horse got shot from under him, only he still managed to bandage the man up and carry him all the way to safety on his back and look after him. That was real brave of him.

## 25th July, Wednesday

There's no one got it today either and thirteen people have been let out of quarantine.

George come over this evening and says he's been to see Lily and told her he can't help having to work so hard in the shop what with plague and them that busy he don't have time to scratch hisself. Only it won't last for ever he says. And in the meantime he's managed to put a bit of money aside. Soon as he can take some time off, they can be married if it's still all right with her. It seems Lily said yes. So they're ENGAGED. I'm that excited. So is Maisie. Only Ma had to sit down when she heard. She got such a shock. She always said she thought we'd get married in line: Bertie, then George, only Bertie's never been around in one place long enough to get hisself a lady friend to step out with.

## 27th July, Friday

No cases since last Sunday now.

Maisie lost her tooth. Finally. In the end Ma had to tie a piece of cotton round it and yank it out. Pa suggested a big piece of string wound round it and the other end tied to a door knob that somebody shuts sudden. That were too difficult as Maisie wouldn't stand still.

## 26th July, Thursday

Somebody's written a letter in now saying we should call the capital city Wentworth on account of William Charles Wentworth that give us our first constitution. Pa says it's a nice idea and at least he's Australian only it don't sound Australian. But at least it's better than Hopetoun.

## 29th July, Sunday

George and Lily come to see us today and everybody at Ragged School give them a big welcome. Most of them's known George since he were little but Lily come from over Balmain way so they don't know her. They said how lucky George is, she being so pretty and all. She's what Ma calls 'slender' and just like her name with paly gold hair piled up on top.

They don't want to get married straight away but. She wants to get her linen and that together and they'll wait till Bertie gets back so he can be George's best man. It'll give them time to save up a bit more too. But best of all Lily don't have any sisters, only four brothers. So she says me and Maisie can be her bridesmaids. Nothing fancy cos it won't be a big wedding, just best dresses. Only Ma says she got time to put a bit aside and get us something pretty to wear.

## 30 July, Monday

I should have said touch wood cos now somebody else's died of it at North Head.

## 31st July, Tuesday

Western Australia's finally voted YES! They had a referendum and all the miners voted as well and this time there was more people said yes than no.

## 1st August, Wednesday

Today were Maisie's birthday, the same day as the horses. Only Maisie wants to know how come horses get to have theirs on the one day And why's she got to have hers on the same day anyway when I get to share mine with Queen Victoria? But Ma said she didn't plan it that way and if Maisie don't shush up she won't be getting a present. That shut her up quick smart.

Ma and Pa give her a new dolly to make up for Topsy being spoilt even though Maisie won't let Topsy out of her sight since we come to Ragged School. Fred and Artie give her an all day sucker each and I give her a hanky I sewed a bunch of flowers on.

## 2nd August, Thursday

Queen Victoria's son's died. Not the Prince of Wales, her second son who's Prince Alfred. He's also the Duke of Edinburgh and the Duke of Saxe Coburg-Gotha. I wonder if he has to put all that down the bottom of a letter every time he writes one? He was 56, which is old and the paper said he died of a paralysed heart, only he had cancer of the tongue as well.

There's been no plague now for a fortnight.

I wonder if Lord Hopetoun's going to land at Botany Bay like Captain Cook did?

## 3rd August, Friday

Lots of families have left Ragged School now. Specially those as only had their houses cleaned not pulled down. They had to wait for the smell of carbolic to go and for everything to dry out from the steam cleaning and buy new bedding and all that. Now the only ones left are families waiting for new houses to be built.

## 5th August, Sunday

Artie's got chicken pox. There's been a few kids round has it. Me and Fred had it ages ago so we didn't catch it. Artie don't seem too bothered by it but. He's still running

around and out and about in the billycart. With all the
kids cooped up lately as Ma says, you got to expect it.

### 7th August, Tuesday

As well as clean-up gangs in the streets, there's been
scavengers paid to get rubbish out the harbour as well.
They've found 1006 dead rats, 504 dogs, 300 chooks and
279 cats. There's also been pigs and sheep and other
animals in the harbour and more than a hundred pieces of
meat. You can imagine what it were like. No wonder you
could hardly see the colour of the water for dirt.

### 8th August, Wednesday

There's been no one come down with plague now for
three weeks. Touch wood again but. Only there's still a
man very sick with it at North Head. The cemetery there
must be nearly full by now with all the people that's died.

### 10th August, Friday

Too soon. There's been another one, someone called William
Montague turned up at Sydney Hospital feeling crook, only
they got suspicious and sent him off to North Head.

Ma saved me this bit from the paper today. There's a Frenchman with a fancy name, Prince Henri of Orleans, who can skip. At least he took a holiday on board ship and did skipping for exercise. Every morning he got up real early and went up on deck in his pyjamas before the ladies come up.

Only to skip you got to keep your feet together and on ship you got to keep them apart, specially if it's rolling so you don't fall over. So somehow he had to skip with his feet apart and together at the same time. Of course it didn't work. And the rope he had were heavy and covered in tar so he kept hitting hisself with it. Then one day he landed flat on his back on deck and everyone looking. He were that embarrassed lying there in his pyjamas, he give up skipping all together.

It's ages since I've done any skipping. Every time I go looking for my rope I find Maisie or one of the boys is using it so it don't seem much point.

**14th August, Wednesday**

Dolly had a meeting with the matron at Sydney Hospital today. She were there for ages, she said, with the matron asking her questions. She wanted to know if Dolly just liked the idea of being a nurse and maybe the uniform and putting flowers in vases. Only Dolly said she knew it were really long hours and scrubbing floors and scouring bedpans and she didn't mind hard work. And she didn't mind having to live in, and anyway, anything was better than sticking labels on jars. She told the matron even if she didn't get to pass the exam she still wanted to try and the matron said she'd think about it and let Dolly know.

### 16th August, Thursday

Maisie come down with chicken pox today and Eddy yesterday. Reggie had it when I did so he's all right. But Maisie's fair covered in them. All over her chest, poor little mite, and back and some on her face as well. She keeps grizzling on account of the itch and Ma's had to put her hands in socks to stop her from scratching cos she didn't have no proper mittens. We've all told her if she scratches the spots on her face she'll end up with dents that'll be there for ever and she won't look nearly so pretty. That just makes her grizzle all the more. She's got it much worse than Artie but.

### 17th August, Friday

There's been Australians fighting somewhere in Africa called Elands River. Pa come back from the Herald office and told us. He says they was meant to relieve this town called Rustenburg the Boers were attacking. They hadn't even got that far when Colonel Baden-Powell tell them to go back again to the camp at Elands River only to make sure the road to Rustenberg were safe to get supplies through.

All the time they could hear the guns booming as the Boers shelled the town. Then suddenly there's other Boers coming up on all the hills either side firing on the road and horses stampeding all over the place terrified, those that haven't been killed or injured.

Just then more troopers arrive and somehow they manage to get back to camp. Next day they're meant to go to Mafeking only during the night the Boers bring in more men and, come daylight, they start firing on the camp. There's New South Bushmen, Queensland Mounteds and Victorians inside as well as Rhodesians, about five hundred all up, as well as African drivers and Boer families that have surrendered and come in with their horses and cattle. All around the camp there's 3000 Boers firing on them. They managed to stick it out for thirteen days till finally Lord Kitchener comes riding up with a whole lot more troops and the Boers took off.

**19th August, Sunday**

Bertie's written to Pa now. He says over there they don't think of themselves as New South Welsh or Victorians or Tasmanians. They're just Australians, fighting in the British army.

Miss Nunn's sick with flu. I don't know how Miss Collins is going to cope with her class as well as her own.

## 20th August, Monday

Miss Collins asked Ma to help today with the little kids,
just keep them busy she said, reading them stories and
helping them with writing. Ma loved it. She gets on well
with little kids and is ever so patient when she has to be
and, with their reading, she knows how hard it is now.

There's been no plague at all since the 9th of August
and people are finally starting to say it's over.

## 25th August, Saturday

George's birthday today, only he couldn't come round to
see us on account of he's not had chicken pox and don't
want to get it now. Ma says he somehow missed out
getting it between Bertie and Ethel and if a grown-up gets
it they come down a lot worse. So he and Lily have gone
over to her parents' for his birthday tea.

## 27th August, Monday

There's only three people sick left at North Head now.

I've finally said yes to Reggie that I'll be his
valentine. Only it's a secret. Fred and Artie would only
go blurting it out to Ma and she'll probably say I wasn't
to be anyone's valentine. I'm still too young. But I don't
think I am.

## 28th August, Tuesday

The rat-catchers are still finding some to catch but not near so many. They used to get 900 a day when things were really bad, only now they get about 350. That's still a lot of rats when you see them piled up only we don't see them lying around dead any more.

The paper says there's been 71 000 disposed of since the start, and 103 humans dead from plague.

## 29th August, Wednesday

Dolly's had a letter back from the matron saying if she's still keen at the end of the year then the matron will have her starting next year. Dolly's not given notice at the factory yet. Pa says November's time enough for that.

## 30th August, Thursday

Pa's told Ma they can afford a two-up two-downer this time. They'll start building first thing Monday morning. He'll help too now clean-up's finished. He's not a carpenter so he'll only get labourer's wages, but that's still 7 shillings a day and, as Ma says, it's better than a poke in the eye with a blunt stick. This way Pa says it'll get done much faster and any time Fred's not in school and weekends he can help too.

### 31st August, Friday

No cases for a whole month and no more rats round either and there's new houses going up in the streets that's cleared. And only 122 days to Federation!

### 3rd September, Monday

They've started! Not that there's much to see yet. They only measured up the ground and marked it out. Reggie and his family will still be living next door. I'm so glad

### 5th September, Wednesday

Artie asked Pa today what difference will it make when we get Federation and Pa said there'll be things like postage stamps all being same, not different for each colony. And there'll be one army, not six. And Fred asked will the railway lines be all the same size only Pa weren't sure about that. Not at first anyway, maybe one day.

## 7th September, Friday

Ma took herself off to St Mary's today to see it dedicated.
She said there were bishops from other colonies there,
looking ever so splendid, even from as far away as New
Zealand. She just sat up the back and watched them all
and listened to all the lovely music. Fred's studied all the
measurements and he's told Pa the tower is 127 foot high
and when they build the ones down the far end, they'll be
232 feet. Only Pa said it'll be a long while before they
have the money to build them.

## 9th September, Sunday

Artie wants to know if we'll be getting a new flag for
Federation and Pa scratched his head and said he didn't
know. He says we'll have the Union Jack to start with but
after that maybe they'll hold a competition to get a new one.
    We can see the foundations now and the carpenters'll
start tomorrow. Then come the brickies. Every afternoon
as soon as school's finished Fred's round there helping Pa.

## 12th September, Wednesday

There's more horses waiting down at Darling Harbour
ready for shipping to South Africa. It's because there've
been so many die I expect. It's just don't seem fair.

## 14th September, Friday

Pa's birthday today. He's been that happy this year what with clean-up and now the house going up and being able to put a bit of money aside. Last night I heard him telling Ma he should have enough to put a deposit on another cart and horse if they're not too dear and he can find somewhere to stable the horse. Ma says he's done so well for himself that, first chance she gets, she's going to buy him a set of them £2.10 teeth they had advertised. That'll be his birthday present from her and he deserves them.

## 15th September, Saturday

There's nothing been done about celebrations yet for Federation. There's not even a committee set up and Ma says they'd better get a move on otherwise there'll be nothing ready. Only 107 days to go.

## 17th September, Monday

The Queen's going to give us the table and inkstand she used to sign the paper. She's sending them out as a present, only they're on show now in England for people to look at before they come out. There's been two thousand seen them so far.

## 18th September, Tuesday

There's been another meeting to get women the vote and Sir William Lyne has promised he'll do everything he can to get the bill through. The women say it's all right for them to send their sons off to war only they can't vote any more than criminals or people in asylums can. What's the good of having Federation, they say, if women can't vote in it?

I don't know why the Premier's been made Sir William. It's not as if he's done anything special, only Pa says members of parliament often get made Sirs.

## 19th September, Wednesday

Mr Kruger's going to leave South Africa in a warship and go and live in Holland where they've said he can stay.

The Queen's sending her grandson, the Duke of York, out to Australia to open up the new parliament next year. And she's put a notice in the London Gazette saying, 'On or after January 1, 1901 the six Federating Colonies of Australia will be united under the name of the Commonwealth of Australia.' New Zealand's been invited to be part of Federation but they're not sure they want to be.

## 22nd September, Saturday

Ma was reading out the adverts today and come across one for a kangaroo. Female and perfectly tame and going cheap. 'Well I never,' says Ma. 'Fancy anyone keeping a kangaroo in Bondi.' Only straight away Maisie wants to know if she can have it.

'No Maisie,' Ma says real firm. 'No horses, no dogs and NO kangaroos. The poor thing'd have to jump up and down on the spot.'

Then Maisie starts to sniff and the tears start coming and Ma gives her a cuddle and says, 'I tell you what. I'll take you and Artie up town to Victoria Markets to see the birds. Would you like that?'

Maisie stops sniffing and it looks like it's on the tip of her tongue to ask if she can have one, when Ma says, 'No you can't but soon as we get our new house, I'll let you have a kitten. Will that do?'

Maisie give Ma this big smile. Maybe when it's bigger it'll be a help to keep any rats away.

## 24th September, Monday

I went for a walk with Reggie yesterday. We had to take Maise and Eddy with us. We headed up Observatory Hill and let them run round while we sat on the bench and held hands. Only every time Maisie or Eddy come near us we had to let go in case they told at home.

Mr Ah Han come round today for the first time since

plague broke out. Ma happened to spot him in Kent Street with his dray all loaded up and said she were real pleased to see him again. They chatted for a bit and he said the plague almost ruined him. He lost all his customers when he couldn't get to them, and now he's having to start all over again. He said some had come back but there's others won't have nothing to do with him on account of he's Chinese. Ma said they weren't worth having, and she'd spread the word he's back and make sure he gets plenty of customers. And Mr Han grinned and said, 'Thank you, Missy.' He always calls her Missy. I think she rather likes it. It makes her feel young again.

### 26th September, Wednesday

They're thinking of holding a competition for a Commonwealth ode and all the colonies will put in £50 pounds to make up a decent prize.

The new parliament is going to meet in Melbourne till we get a federal capital site and a parliament house built on it, only Pa says that could take years. In the meantime but Melbourne says we can have their Exhibition Buildings once they've fixed them up.

### 27th September, Thursday

Lord Roberts has just turned 68. That really is old. I expect he's looking forward to finishing the war and going home.

## 28th September, Friday

Ma and me went up town today to see what beds and tables and chairs cost since ours were all smashed during clean-up.

I love going up town. Not that our part of town isn't busy, that's when things are normal, what with wharves and ships and all. But up town there's always carts and drays and wagons and men in waistcoats with their shirt-sleeves rolled up like they're trying to look even busier. And the fancy gents' carriages going past and ladies stepping across the road in their smart hats. Only my favourites are hansom cabs lined up on the side waiting for passengers, while the drivers have a bit of a kip and the horses get to feed from their nosebags. It always seems somehow quiet, coming back home again.

Most of the toffs' shops had furniture too dear but Ma's says there's plenty of places over Glebe and Surry Hills got furniture and she'll find something. This time she's determined we'll have beds to sleep in even if we have to share for a bit longer.

## 29th September, Saturday

The French and Germans have been trying out motor cars to use in their armies. That means they wouldn't need to use horses and I think that's a very good idea and somebody should tell the British.

Only 92 days left to Federation now.

### 1st October, Monday

The Minister for Education's thinking of giving every
school child a medal for Federation. I'd like that and
Reggie can't wait. He says it'll be the first medal he's
ever had. Specially since I wouldn't let him join up.

### 2nd October, Tuesday

Mr Oliver says a hundred and twenty-five square miles
won't be big enough for a capital city after all so that
ruled out some places he's looked at. And there's other
things, like enough water. You don't have to have a butter
factory but.

They've brung in this new rule in the war. Any Boers
found wearing British uniforms will be shot straight
away. I asked Pa why would they want to wear our
uniforms when they've got their own clothes. Only he
said they could be pretending to be British soldiers or
maybe their own clothes have just worn out.

### 8th October, Monday

Pa says it's not up to Mr Oliver to say where to put the
capital city. He just has to tell the government places
worth looking at. Now it's up to the members of
parliament to decide. So he says they're fixing up a

couple of railways carriages for eating and sleeping in because there's nowhere out in the middle of the country for the MPs to stay.

### 9th October, Tuesday

Reggie and me are getting worried now there won't be anything organised for Federation. There's still not even a committee and nobody knows where the Governor-General's going to land. Reggie thinks maybe we should get all the kids we know from round here to put up streamers at least otherwise there won't be anything on the day.

### 10th October, Wednesday

Pa says wherever they decide to put the capital city, they'll have to buy the land from the farmers.

Artie said, 'Why? The farmers didn't buy it from the Aborigines.'

Pa said that were different. Only Artie can't see why but.

Fred's back molars are coming through. His mouth's that sore he can hardly eat and, given how much he eats, that must be hard. He has to wait till his soup cools down before he eats it. He's a good kid but. You never hear him complain about it.

Pa says there's a grasshopper plague way out west.
Condobolin.

Maisie says, 'What's a grasshopper?'

Pa says, 'You mean to tell me you don't know what a
grasshopper is ?'

Ma reminded him all us kids was born in the Rocks
and there aren't that many grasshoppers round. So Pa
tells Maisie that thousands and thousands of little hoppers
get on the farmers' crops and eat everything, right down
to the stalks till there's nothing left.

Then he says how come she knows what a kangaroo
is, only she don't know what a grasshopper is. There
aren't many roos round the Rocks neither. Only Maisie
says Miss Nunn's showed them a picture of a kangaroo
and lion on the New South Wales crest.

There's other women holding meetings now because they
don't want the vote. Ma says they should make up their
mind. They say it'll mean families won't agree and
women should stick to the things they know like homes
and babies. Ma's as mad as a snake over it. 'I got just as
much right to say what I think as Pa does. And if I ever
get to vote I will.'

## 13th October, Saturday

Someone's written to *The Herald* to say Sir Henry Parkes' grave is all run down and overgrown. That's a real shame Pa said. He started the whole idea of Federation and even thought up the name 'Commonwealth'. I hope they get it fixed up in time.

Only 79 days still to go.

## 14th October, Sunday

Ma says there's all these adverts in for French millinery and I said, 'You mean to wear with your heliotrope blouse from Paris and the Princess pearl clasp?'

'Something like that,' says Ma. Then Maisie wants to know what millinery is.

'Hats,' Ma tells her, 'for ladies to wear to the races. The Melbourne Cup'll be on soon.The adverts say you can get parasols for the sun and lace capes and dust capes and gloves and lisse ruffles for skirts, even artistic underwear.'

And straight away Artie pipes up, 'What's artistic underwear, Ma?'

And Ma says that's none of his business.

## 16th October, Tuesday

There's lots of artists and architects have designed things for decorations only nobody knows if we'll be having one even. The government can't even decide where to hold the official ceremony. If they make it Circular Quay they can maybe put up a couple of thousand seats. If they have it in front of Government House they could put up a pavilion. And if they hold it in Centennial Park they can easily fit in a hundred thousand people. That's the best idea by far, Pa says.

But how's the Governor-General going to arrive? That's what I want to know. If he comes in at Circular Quay, it could be on a barge. If it's at Government House, he's only got to step out of his front door. Only at Centennial Park he could arrive in a fancy carriage and at least that way all the people would get to see him.

Ma says if they don't get a move on his Lordship won't be going nowhere on the day and all he'll get is a cup of tea and a biscuit if he's lucky.

## 18th October, Thursday

It were a heatwave today after days and days of really cold weather. I hope if it goes on like this the rats don't come back. Maybe they won't know it's all been cleaned up.

Reggie and me been round to all the school kids we know and we think we could each make about fifty decorations each. Just cut up paper, painted and glued together. Still if all of us made fifty and we stuck it all together it'd maybe spread out for quite a bit round Dawes Point.

### 20th October, Saturday

New Zealand still don't know about Federation. Their Premier's putting it to the parliament to get them to decide. They'd better make up their minds soon but.

### 22nd October, Monday

The army says it wants 300 000 pounds of jam sent to South Africa. How can anyone eat that much? Pa says there'll have to be more than one factory supplies it so I hope Dolly's gets to, specially their dark plum.

### 23rd October, Tuesday

Now the army says it wants 100 000 tons of potatoes as well and they're willing to pay £9 a ton for them.

'That's a lot of spuds, Pa,' says Artie. 'How many baked taters would that be?'

Pa says, 'No idea, but how much does it come to?'

Fred says, '£900 000. Only how many rats would you have to find to get that much.'

'More than you're ever going to find,' says Pa. 'But never mind you got a good head on your shoulders.'

At last, there's a committee been set up to do the decorations. So Reggie and me don't have to get all the kids round the Rocks making streamers which is a relief I can tell you. I was wondering what Ma would have to say when I set up making them on her new table.

There'll be a big procession and festivities planned for a whole week. And a carnival on the harbour with all the ships decorated. Then there'll be a choir of school kids and horse races and cricket matches and fireworks at night of course. There's twenty-five members on the committee. They got £20 000 to spend. That's twice as much as the lights in Dublin cost when the Queen paid a visit.

### 25th October, Thursday

There was a big fire out on the harbour last night. The steam ferry, *Kangaroo*, went up in flames over near Lavender Bay. We woke up when we heard the fire engines and Pa took me and Fred and Artie down to Dawes Point to see it. Reggie and his pa were there too. They think it must have started about 10 only there was no sign of fire before then. Mr Cook said it was probably below decks but before they knew it the whole boat was in flames from end to end. Artie said, 'It's just like fireworks, only better,' and Pa said he weren't to talk like that because no one could save it.

The fire brigade from North Sydney come down but had to keep pulling their hoses off the tracks whenever a train come past and all the passengers were hanging out the window for a look. A fire engine come from Circular Quay too and both of them poured water at it, only they couldn't get close enough to stop the flames. It were police boats and steam ferries in the end that stopped it cos they could get in close.

On the way back Reggie and me started walking real slow while the others went on ahead. Next thing Reggie's grabbed my hand and is squeezing. Just then Pa turns round and I think he sees us, only all he says is, 'Hey, you two snails. Get a move on or we'll lose you.'

### 26th October, Friday

Mr Oliver's looked at twenty-three places for a capital city and says there's only three worth considering. That's Monaro, Orange and Yass-Canberra. Now all we have to do is wait for the MPs to make up their minds, whenever that'll be.

### 27th October, Saturday

The government's been asking other countries could they maybe send troops to march in our parade for Federation. The Viceroy of India's sending a hundred officers and horses and the Queen says she'll send some of her household cavalry.

## 29th October, Monday

Pa went down to the Herald today to check up on the
latest on the war. He says there's always crowds looking
at the photos and the big map that shows where the
troopers are now. New South Mounteds have captured
two Krupp guns and four wagons at a place called
Rensburg Drift. Reggie says Krupps are the big guns
made by the Germans.

## 31st October, Wednesday

Queen Victoria's grandson favourite has died in South
Africa. Not the one coming out to open our parliament.
Prince Christian Victor of Schleswig-Holstein. He died of
typhoid in hospital in Pretoria. It makes you think but,
just how lucky Bertie was. The Queen's very old and her
health's not good, and this has left her feeling very down.

Mrs Kruger's still in Pretoria. Isn't that odd? Wouldn't
you think he'd have taken her with him to Holland.
Anyway he's sent a message telling her to trust in the
Lord and look up Psalm 91. You'd think he would have
said something a bit more friendly.

## 1st November, Thursday

Our house is ready to move in. Monday. There's teams of men out working on houses as fast as they can and you can see the rows going up either side of streets where the old houses were before. And not dumped higgledy-piggledy one on top of the other either. Ma can't wait. She's tired of the hall and looking forward to having her own kitchen and wash house again.

## 2nd November, Friday

The plague may be over but Pa says there'll be some people that's never the same again. Some families lost their breadwinner and now there's no money coming in. Others lost a mother and there's little ones without someone to care for them. And all those people that lost businesses, when someone died or no one would go near them after. You can still see shops closed that haven't opened again.

The Paines have picked up again, but I wonder what happened to Mrs Dudley. Her children were all grown up so they'd be all right. She used to be a teacher back in England, but that were a long time ago. And there must be lots of others we'll never know what happened.

## 3rd November, Saturday

The Premier plans to take back the land from George to
Fort Street as far as Princes, then from Charlotte Place to
Argyle Street. It's not as if it's a nice area he says.
There've been rookeries crammed in there from the very
early days. But with wider streets and bits of park it will
look really good for Federation. But Ma says what right's
Sir William got talking about rookeries as if we was
perched like seagulls where we had no business to be.
She says it's all very well for him in his fancy house
talking like that. Round the Rocks we don't always get
the chance to choose where we live.

Only 58 days to Federation.

## 5th November, Monday

We've moved in! Today! Miss Collins let us have the day
off school and we spent the morning carrying bundles of
clothing and pots and pans and bedding up from
Harrington Street. Then the table Ma bought come this
afternoon and the chairs. The beds'll be here Thursday.
None of us minded but, we've been sleeping on the floor
for so long now what does a couple more nights matter,
specially when it's in our own house. Maisie and Artie
spent the whole time running up and down the stairs till
Ma said if they didn't stop she'd send them straight back
to Ragged School and they could live there permanent.
But come bedtime they were so worn out they went

straight off to sleep without a peep out of either.

### 6th November, Tuesday

Melbourne Cup today. There were twenty-seven horses
supposed to run only Pa said that were too many, there'd be
some scratched for sure. He read out all the names and
Maisie said she wanted Bride only I said maybe Grizzle
would be better. Ma told me to hush up. Artie wanted Wait-
a-bit cos he's slower than Fred and always having to catch
up. Anyway Pa said he'd shout us each a tanner to see if we
could pick the winner and he'd be bookie. So we wrote
down the names of our horses on bits of paper. Ma and me
had the favourites, Lancaster and Severity. We won't know
till tomorrow's paper what won so we'll just have to wait.

### 7th November, Wednesday

The favourites came nowhere. None of the horses we
picked even got a place so we lost, only when Pa come in
tonight with the paper he had this big grin on his face,
wide as wide, and said he'd picked the winner.

'What won?' we all said at once.

'Clean Sweep,' said Pa. 'What else?'

Seems he didn't know nothing about this horse, only
it sounded good what with all the cleaning-up he's seen.
'It were 20–1 too,' he said, only he wouldn't tell Ma how
much he'd put on even though Fred was dying to know.

Ma looked cross and said we didn't have the money to spare for horse racing.

Pa said, 'But, Ma, this is the Cup. That's different. It's only once a year.' Then he whispered in her ear how much he'd won. She said, 'That much!' Then she got a grin almost as wide as his. Then he said next Saturday he's going to take us all over to Manly for the day.

Guess what? Reggie's coming to Manly. Because he and his pa helped on our house, Pa wants to take him with us. I'm ever so pleased only I didn't say so to Pa. They don't know about Reggie and me.

### 9th November, Friday

Pa gave Ma some money to take us up town and buy us some new clothes. The boys' pants are almost worn through and I've grown so much the last few months all my old dresses are too short. Ma said I needed something half decent to cover my legs. So she bought me two dresses, one for best. It's real pretty, white with pin-tucking on the bodice and cotton lace on the sleeves and it comes right down to touch the top of my boots. And I got a hat to go with it. Only Ma says to make sure it don't blow off into the water cos she'll not be buying me another.

I'm tired out but there's no chance I'll sleep yet. I'm still that worked up after our day out. Ma were going to make sandwiches for us to eat on the beach but Pa said no need for that, he had everything planned.

Reggie come over about half past nine and we walked down to Circular Quay. Pa paid 6d for him and Ma, 3d each for us kids. Soon we were sitting out on the deck in the sun and the man's loosened the ropes and he's pulling the gangway in and we're on our way.

Pa had to shout at Freddy to get him away from the railing and Reggie held on to Artie when he tried to lean right out but Maisie wouldn't leave Ma's side all the way over, saying it were bumpy. It were nothing of the sort, just gentle up and down. Much nicer than the launch over to quarantine.

When we got to Manly wharf we had to walk up the street to get to the beach the other side and there's all these pine trees, some quite tall, others not long planted and this lovely stretch of white white sand, only it's packed with people already. You have to look hard for a bit just to sit down. Ma brung a blanket and Pa spread it out and Fred and Artie started right in making sandcastles.

There was people paddling and soon as Fred saw them he and Artie had their boots off and they're running down to the water. Before you know it they're up to their knees in it and Ma's yelling if a wave come and dump them they got no other clothes to go home in. Maisie just wanted to build sandcastles and go nowhere near the water except for a bit to pour in her moat. Reggie helped her build a castle that were quite grand with a drawbridge and all.

Then next thing he asks if I want to go paddling. Ma give me a funny look and says I better change behind her. So I take off me boots and black stockings and we run down the water. It's so cold at first it give me a shock but lovely when you get used to it. Only I have to hold my skirt up so it don't get wet, all the time making sure my drawers aren't showing, even if they are my best pair that Ma sewed lace on. But Reggie's being ever so gentlemanly and holding my hand only so's I don't fall over in the water. He never once looks at me legs. Only that's probably because he knows Ma's watching him with hawk eyes from up the beach.

Anyway next thing Pa's calling it's time we tidied up and find one of them fancy tea shops for sandwiches and lemonade. He and Ma are dying for a cup of tea really. While the boys get their boots back on I hide behind Ma and wriggle back into me stockings and boots.

Then after lunch we go for this long walk right along the beach and Pa and the boys are out in front. Then comes Ma with Maisie, then me and Reggie lagging behind. Reggie don't dare take my hand in broad daylight but. Not with Ma there.

When it starts to get late we head back to catch the ferry home. And Reggie and me move to sit up the front. Next thing the wind's blown my new hat off and it lands on the deck and is just about to blow over when Reggie grabs it. Ma were cross with me when she heard for not hanging onto it, only ever so pleased with Reggie for saving it.

Then we come back into Circular Quay and walk

slowly back up the hill home. And even though Maisie wanted Pa to carry her he said he were much too tired and this were one time she had to walk.

## 12th November, Monday

Mr Ah Han come round again today. Ma's been able to talk a few people back into being customers, telling them the plague had nothing to do with him and he says business is starting to pick up again. Slow.

## 13th November, Tuesday

Pa come home tonight and said he had a surprise for Maisie only she had to guess. But just then there's a tiny mew come from his coat pocket and it wriggles.

Maisie yells, 'Me kitten!'

Pa hands her this tiny little fluff ball all stripy just like a tiger. Seems Elsie and Jess's pa knew someone as was trying to find homes for kittens and they took one. Reggie's pa's got one for Eddy.

Straight away Maisie picks it up and hugs it tight and Ma has to tell her it's only little and to be gentle. Then Artie wants a nurse and then Fred. So by the time Tommy—that's his name—got to bed in a box Pa's fixed up in the kitchen, he's fair worn out.

## 15th November, Thursday

The army says it wants more jam.

Ma said, 'What on earth for?'

I says, 'They must be making jam tarts and roly-polys for afternoon tea.'

Maisie and Eddy played kittens today. She says you can't play dollies with a boy, only kittens is fine.

## 17th November, Saturday

The committee says everything's under control and there'll be decorations and illuminations and things like cycling and athletics and music and theatre programmes.

They're even thinking of putting up a big statue on Fort Denison to show Australia Facing The Dawn. It'd have a lady looking out to sea and round her skirt there'd be little navigators and explorers like Captain Cook and Flinders and Stuart and Burke and Wills. Artie asked if there'd be any Aborigines round her too, only Pa says the government don't usually put them on statues.

There's 44 days to go still.

## 22nd November, Thursday

It's funny to think that all over Australia there are people getting ready for Federation. In country towns as well as big cities. And there's been sixty odes sent in to the competition as well as anthems and songs for children to sing on the day. And anyone that comes to Sydney will easily find somewhere to stay and they're making railway tickets cheaper specially.

## 23rd November, Friday

Lord Hopetoun's been sick with fever. So's her ladyship.

I said, 'Does that mean they got the plague?'

Pa says it's more likely they got malaria, on account of they been to places like Ceylon where there's plenty of mosquitoes.

## 25th November, Sunday

Dolly come over today and said she's more certain than ever she wants to go nursing. She's writing to tell the matron she hasn't changed her mind and soon as the matron says yes she'll tell her manager. There's always girls looking for jobs so it shouldn't be hard for him to replace her. And Ethel says she'll find someone else to board with when Dolly has to live in.

## 29th November, Thursday

Lord Roberts is now on his way back to England. He says there's not much left to do in the war and he's left the tidying up to Lord Kitchener who'll be in charge of the army from now on.

Bertie's written to Pa telling him he's sick of being on the move the whole time. The long marches are starting to get to him and soon as he's back he plans to find himself a job in Sydney and stay put. No more wandering. Ma's delighted, so am I. We both miss Bertie. He's always good for a laugh, only Ma says he can come home for a bit but then has to find his own place. We may have a two up two downer now, but it'll start getting pretty cramped if Bertie moves in.

## 1st December, Saturday

There's going to be a Triumphal Arch over Pitt Street and at night everything'll be lit up with bulbs. The Garden Palace Gardens and the Domain and Hyde Park even. Streets like Macquarie and Hunter will be lit too and Queen Square and Martin Place, then they'll go right up Oxford Street. Then over in Moore Park there'll be flagpoles up with lights strung between them.

Ma got a letter today from Mrs Alexander. She does have lovely handwriting. She said she's buying herself a new sewing machine and would Ma like her old one? It's a good treadle and hardly used and Ma said, 'Would I ever! She must have read me mind,' and she's writing back straight away to say yes please.

### 4th December, Tuesday

There'll be arches in Park and College Streets and in Elizabeth and that's not counting all the bunting and streamers that's going up now.

There's been no more talk of medals but every school kid's to get a parchment with their name on it. It don't sound too bad only Reggie and I would rather have a medal.

### 7th December, Friday

We broke up for school holidays today and I felt really sad because it were my last day at Ragged School. Ma and Pa come to see our concert where we sang carols and Fred and I got certificates for Good Work. Then Miss Collins talked to the parents and told them all the things we'd done this year and how I'd won the essay prize. I could feel meself going red in front of all the parents and visitors. Only then she had me stand up and say a poem I'd learnt specially. She let me choose meself and I didn't want to learn one of them long poems about burning ships. So I chose this one. It's called, 'What Became of Them?'

*He was a rat, and she was a rat,*
*And down in one hole they did dwell,*
*And both were as black as a witch's cat,*
*And they loved one another well.*

*He had a tail, and she had a tail,*
*Both long and curling and fine;*
*And each said, 'Yours is the finest tail*
*In the world, excepting mine.'*

*He smelt the cheese, and she smelt the cheese,*
*And they both pronounced it good;*
*And both remarked it would greatly add*
*To the charms of their daily food.*

*So he ventured out, and she ventured out,*
*And I saw them go with pain;*
*But what befell them I never can tell,*
*For they never came back again!*

When I finished everybody clapped and laughed and
said Hear, hear! because we're all tired of rats and don't
ever want to see one again. After it were over I said
good-bye to Miss Collins and thanked her for giving me
my diary what won me the prize and she made me
promise to go in and see her every now and then and tell
her what I'm doing.

## 13th December, Thursday

There'll be flags from all different nations flying and
10 000 kids singing in Centennial Park.

There's only 17 days to go now.

## 14th December, Friday

Mr Ah Han asked us all over for tea tonight. Not at his
house, to a restaurant in Wexford Street just opened
called Ma Sun's. We'd never had Chinese food before
and Maisie whispered to Pa it looked funny. Only Pa said
you should always eat what's put in front of you. So
Maisie didn't say nothing only tried it and ate it all up! It
were really nice. Different, but nice. Mr Ah Han and his
wife were there and Soo and Li who say they can skip
really fast now. And Mr Ah Han said he wanted to say
thank you to us for being nice when all that bad business
were happening.

## 15th December, Saturday

Ma heard from Bertie this week. She'd written to say she
could read now and he wrote back and said how pleased
he is for her.

He said tell Pa if he wants to go back in the rag and bone
business he's more than happy to go in with him and he

promises to find somewhere to board soon as he can.

I've just had this wonderful idea. I'm going to introduce Bertie to Miss Collins. She knows all about him cos I've showed her his letters and told her all about him and I'm sure she'd like him. And Bertie will love her for sure.

### 16th December, Sunday

Ethel come over today with Albert. It seems now they're planning to get married next year too only not till much later. In the meantime she says Albert's sister's got a job in town lined up and she'll move into the boarding house soon as Dolly moves out. Dolly starts on the 2nd of January. Ma says it's all happening too fast. She can't hardly keep up with us. The only good thing about it is with any luck she'll be able to wear the same outfit to both George and Ethel's weddings and save a bit that way.

### 17th December, Monday

New Zealand won't be part of Federation after all. They've decided. I can understand that. There's a whole sea between us, so that makes them another country, not like Western Australia which is just over the other side of the same country.

## 18th December, Tuesday

George come round today to tell us his boss give him a bonus for Christmas because of how hard he's worked this year. And he's made him a junior partner. He'll be putting Barnes up on the sign outside. George just had to tell us. Then he was off to tell Lily as soon as she come out of work.

Lily's a secretary in an office and does typing and shorthand. She's promised to teach me to type over the holidays and I can't hardly wait.

## 20th December, Thursday

There'll be a whole arch covered in wool too only Ma said what a waste when she heard. She said think how many jumpers you could make with it. Pa said it'd be raw wool and not for knitting.

Lord Hopetoun's asked Sir William Lyne to be our first prime minister! He had no right to do that, Pa says. And there's lots of papers saying the same thing. It's all been arranged. Mr Barton's to be our Prime Minister. Anyway Sir William Lyne didn't even want Federation at first so how could he make a good prime minister?

## 21st December, Friday

Mabel says Mr and Mrs Alexander are going to the celebrations. And us and the Cooks are going too. Mabel said they got an official invite. Straight away Artie wants to know if there's a flag on the invite. And Mabel says yes. So he says what's it like? Mabel, who's seen the invite, says, 'It's a white flag with a blue cross down the centre and white stars on it. Oh, and there's a Union Jack up the corner.' So Artie says at least it's got stars on it like the Southern Cross Pa's pointed out to him.

## 22nd December, Saturday

There'll be a wheat arch up in Bridge Street and now all the arches are starting to go up to be ready on time. You can feel the excitement everywhere. It's like everyone's getting ready for a party almost.

9 days.

## 23rd December, Sunday

A cart pulled up outside today and all the kids come round for a look. And there's Mabel with Jim, one of Mrs Alexander's gardeners, with the sewing machine for Ma. Jim wants to know if Pa can help with it. Anyway they get it out and set it up where Ma wants it. Then Jim goes out and brings in this big basket full of things like a pudding and ham and a couple of chooks the cook's done specially, and mince pies and all sorts of things, even jars of lollies I can see Artie got his eye on.

Ma were quite overcome and didn't know what to say only Mabel tells her Mrs Alexander said to say she were that pleased with Mabel she just wanted to say thank you to her family. Ma had to sit down for a bit. She's not used to people doing things like that for her. So I put the kettle on and asked Jim if he'd maybe like a cup of tea, so they stayed on for a bit. That way we got to talk to Mabel till it were time to go back.

### 24th December, Monday

It's definitely Mr Barton for Prime Minister. Nobody wanted Sir William, even if he is Premier. Pa couldn't be more pleased. He's always liked Mr Barton and says he'll be much better than Sir William, whatever Lord Hopetoun says.

I've made Maisie's new doll a dress for Christmas and I'm giving her my skipping rope to keep. She's usually got it tied to her basket anyway.

### 25th December, Tuesday

I thought we'd be having Christmas in our new house only Ma said it'd be a pity to waste the picnic hamper. Besides she only had chairs for us, let alone the rest of the family.

Since it were a warm day we went up the Botanic Gardens. And there was George and Lily, Ethel and Albert, Dolly, me, Fred, Artie and Maisie and Ma and Pa. The only two missing were Mabel and Bertie but as Ma says you never get things perfect, only nearly.

We found a lovely spot with a bit of shade so Ma didn't get too hot and spread out a couple of blankets and Ma said she couldn't remember a nicer Christmas what with how lucky we'd been this year considering. And Pa said just as well Bertie weren't here cos if he's been on half rations all this time he'd probably eat the lot. Everyone laughed.

### 26th December, Wednesday

I forgot to tell my news. Pa and Ma give me a typewriter for Christmas! Not new, but still good. Pa rang the manager of the jam factory to ask where he could get one a bit cheaper. The manager said he were getting a new one for the office and he could let him have the old one for less than half. Pa says I still got to finish school and do my Junior, only this'll do for practice on in the meantime.

### 27th December, Thursday

Ma says soon as the sales come on she's going to buy herself something smart for the weddings. She'll look out for some pretty material to make dresses for Maisie and me to wear.

The government wants every one to have a good time for Commonwealth Day. So any families that's poor and needy can get food from particular grocers for the week. And them that don't have homes'll get tickets that give them two meals a day for the whole week. So that's good.

### 29th December, Saturday

I've had my first lesson on my typewriter. The keys stand up quite high, only Lily covered them over and made me look at a chart of the letters, so I get to feel where they are. Then I have to think of a line down the middle and each finger with its row of letters to hit. The little fingers have two rows each and that's hard because they're not so strong as the others but Lily says it'll come with practice. A bit like Ma and her reading.

### 30th December, Sunday

'You've always had a mind of your own,' Ma says to me today. 'It must have something to do with red hair.'

I says, 'Yes, Ma, I get from you.'

She laughs and say, 'Probably.'

Ma said we could stay up tonight, even Maisie, because it was special, not like any New Year. I don't s'pose anyone in Sydney went to bed early. A good big moon was up and everything so still you could hear the sound of boat parties floating back over the water. And all the houses across the other side had their gardens lit with Chinese lanterns.

Straight after tea we set off with other families to walk up town past the theatres with all the music and laughing coming from inside what with the doors open and not a spare seat. People were spilling out on the pavement and there were fiddlers and accordions playing on almost every corner. The churches kept open too, with all these hymns to help welcome in the 20th century.

You could hardly hear one tune above another it was all so loud and as more people come on the streets and everyone began shouting and roaring it got louder still. There were people banging gongs the closer it got to midnight. Reggie was swinging this rattle round and round above his head till his pa told him to watch it or he'd hit someone. Eddy had a whistle that pierced your ears almost and Fred and Artie had sneaked out with Ma's saucepan lids and wooden spoons and kept on banging them till she had a right old headache.

Then right on midnight the church bells chimed and a cheer went up like you've never heard and Reggie grabbed me and kissed me right on the mouth. Ma didn't see thank heavens, because Pa were kissing her. Only Fred did but, and he's got this look like he's bursting to tell her. I say if he knows what's good for him he won't breathe a word.

It's as if the whole country were having its birthday, and it is too. Tomorrow we won't just be separate colonies. We'll be one country, united—a Federation. Then Fred and Artie start banging their saucepan lids even louder.

Then when we get to the end of George Street, we have to turn round and start back again because Maisie and Eddy and the other littlies are getting tired and refuse to walk so the pas hoist them up on their shoulders and they ride back down George Street like elephant tamers. The rest of us have to push our way back through the crowds. Reggie's got me by the hand and won't let go for a minute.

Honestly it's been the best possible New Year's ever!

### 1st January, 1901, Tuesday

Pa even bought a copy of *The Herald* today for us to keep because he said it's special. He's right. Inside there's a copy of the letter the Queen signed, all in fancy printing, and it says, 'Royal Assent to the Commonwealth of Australia Constitution Act 1900 and of her Majesty the Queen's signature, Victoria, by the Queen Herself signed with Her Own Hand.' And up the top corner she's written her name, very neat. Victoria R. That stands for 'Regina' which means 'Queen'. Freddy and me both want to cut it out to keep along with our Federation parchments. Pa says that's not fair there's only one and we're to leave it where everyone can see it. Specially Bertie when he gets back.

*The Herald*'s got no adverts in today only things about Federation and some of the odes. There's one by Mr Brunton-Stephens and another by Mr Roderic Quin. I must say I'm glad I don't have to learn either. There's too many verses.

Pa put it aside to read later there was so much in it, only he said there was one bit that caught his eye. It says there've been thousands of people come to this country to settle and none of it's made much difference to the Aborigines. Pa says he wonders if anyone's bothered to ask them what they thought?

The whole city's dressed up, like it knows it's having a party. Streamers and bunting all along George Street and down the middle poles with big waratahs on them for New South Wales. All the hansoms are gone from Martin Place and they've put poles up with garlands and Union Jacks and up near the top there's a big white pavilion with 'Long Life and Happiness to Lord and Lady Hopetoun' in big letters.

We stood up in Macquarie Street near Bridge with the Cooks right near us. And soon as we heard the noise from the Domain. Fred starts shouting, 'They're coming!' Then the procession comes round and up past Government House gates with two hundred policemen out front ahead of the floats. And there's shearers and miners and stockmen from up country. Pa yells, 'Pity Bertie's not here to see this. It's what he's done.'

After them come fire engines with all the firemen in their shiny brass helmets glinting in the sun and their horses decked out in blue and gold, the colours of the Governor-General. Then come the Italian float with a bust of Sir Henry Parkes and straight after that Lancers on their lovely horses.

Fred and Artie give this big cheer when the New South Wales ride past. There are only some back from the war.

Then New Zealand troopers and the Queen's cavalry in their silver helmets and fluttery plumes and the Indian troopers in their turbans.

As soon as the last of the procession's come past Ma says she's dying for a cup of tea and so is Reggie's ma. They all decide to go home and take the younger ones. Only me and Reggie say please can we go up town to Hyde Park and see it again from there. Ma's about to say no only Pa says, 'Go on let them Ma. It's not as if they're stepping out proper.' Ma says oh all right and Pa says if we run we might catch up to one of the fire engines and get a lift. Then he gives us a tanner each for our fares home and me and Reggie are already wriggling in and out of the crowd as fast as we can to catch the fire engine.

When we reach it Reggie yells out bold as brass, 'Hey, Mister! Will you give us a lift up town?'

I say, 'Please!' on account of Reggie's forgotten his manners and the fireman says, 'Yes but only since your young lady's got manners.'

So there we are me and Reggie riding all the way up Macquarie and along College Street to Hyde Park. Then the fireman says, 'You can stop here if you like or come on up Oxford with us.'

So Reggie and me get to go all the way up Oxford.

And everywhere we look there's people peering out windows and waving from balconies and each side of the street, ten deep easily, cheering all the floats for just about everything. Even the Salvation Army's got one.

Then when we come to Centennial Park we thank them and climb down and head through the big gates and down to where there's this white pavilion with steps covered in red carpet and flowers either side and everything draped with garlands of leaves. Then on the dais there's the table and inkstand the Queen give us for them to sign their names.

And you couldn't imagine the crowds. There must have been seven thousand at least, not counting the ten thousand school kids all in white. Then Lord Hopetoun arrives in his carriage and Lady Hopetoun in hers and all the officials. And Mr Barton's there and Sir William Lyne, only the Governor-General talks to Lady Lyne but doesn't speak to Mr Barton so he's probably still cross.

But he takes the oath and then he has all the Lancers draw their swords and the guns fire 21 times. And the band plays 'God Save the Queen' while everybody stands to attention.

When it were all over Reggie and I walked all the way back down Oxford Street cos we spent our tanners on lollies instead of fares. Ma was a bit cross when I got back late only not when I sat her down and told her about the ceremony.

Then as soon as it got dark, the whole city lit up every big building almost and right across the GPO it said
WELCOME TO OUR GOVERNOR GENERAL
GOD SAVE THE QUEEN
I said to Reggie that if Mr Barton can become Prime

Minister when he come from a family of 11 kids then what's to stop us doing anything we want and Reggie agrees with me.

Reggie's got a bit of money still from clean-up and he's asked me to go ice-skating with him at Prince Alfred Park. Ma will probably say no but he's promised to have me back before dark. I'm hoping she'll maybe let us if we go with Ethel and Albert.

There's a letter come from Bertie saying he'll be coming home the end of March. So that means we can have George and Lily's wedding in April. Bertie'll be so surprised to see how much I've grown and he won't be able to call me chicken legs no more. I'll bet if he tries he'll have Reggie to answer to!

When I'm ready I'm going to write to the manager of the Peacock jam factory and ask if he'll take me on as a junior in the office.

Miss Collins was right. 1900 has been the best year for keeping a diary, only now I've run out of pages so this is where I have to end.

# Historical Note

The year 1900 was an important one in Australia's history. It was the last year of the 19th century and big changes were taking place in the lead up to the 20th. There were some things in particular that affected Australia at that time.

In January 1900, Bubonic plague broke out in Sydney and by August when it disappeared, 103 people had died. There were outbreaks in all other Colonies as well, except Tasmania. The area known as The Rocks in Sydney, which included some appalling slums, was cleaned up at great expense and many buildings were demolished and replaced by new ones. Plague broke out again in Sydney late in 1901 and in 1902 and was a threat for twenty years.

During the epidemic there was strong opposition to the Chinese, sometimes even open hostility and violence. They were held by some people to be 'responsible' for the plague, which was quite untrue. These feelings, however, together with the fear of cheap labour taking away the jobs of white workers, led in 1901 to the White Australia Policy which applied strict restrictions on immigration. This policy did not start to change until the mid-sixties.

Australia was made up of separate, self-governing Colonies, which included New Zealand. Each had its own army, postal system and customs service and all regarded England as the 'Mother Country'. However, there was good sense in combining these services and the fear of being invaded by a foreign power made the thought of 'one people, one destiny' very attractive.

Sir Henry Parkes had been very keen on the idea of Federation but apart from meetings between the Colonies no final decision had been made. By 1900 however, five of the colonies had agreed to Federation, only Western Australia which had voted against it and New Zealand, which was uncertain, still holding back.

In 1900 Australia sent representatives to England to appeal to the British Government to be granted a Federation. The bill had to be passed by both their houses of parliament and the proclamation then signed by Queen Victoria before it could become a reality.

Meanwhile, the gold miners in Western Australia, who had not been given the chance to vote on Federation, demanded the right to do so and another referendum had to be held in that colony. New Zealand referred the matter back to its own parliament for consideration. In the end, Western Australia voted YES and New Zealand voted NO.

The previous year, the Boer War had broken out in South Africa between the Boer and the British peoples. At first there was widespread support from the general public in Australia to supply troops to fight on behalf of Britain and large crowds turned out to wave the troopers goodbye. Different colonies vied with each other to send men, but once in South Africa these troops thought of themselves not as Victorians or Queenslanders but as

Australians. After January 1, 1901 when Federation was declared and there was one army for the whole country, all soldiers sent from Australia went as Australians.

Commonwealth troops usually fought as units attached to the British Army. However, in one engagement, in August 1900, about 500 soldiers, mostly Australians, were surrounded by 3000 Boers at Elands River Post. They managed to hold out for 13 days under heavy fire, before help could arrive.

During 1900 a search was begun to find a suitable site for a federal capital city. New South Wales and Victoria as the two most powerful colonies had agreed that the capital should be between Sydney and Melbourne but no less than 100 miles from Sydney. Three sites were suggested as suitable but it was not until 1908 that the members of parliament agree on one. That site was not named Canberra until 1913.

Until then, the Federal Parliament met in Melbourne. It was opened in May 1901 by the Duke of York, a grandson of Queen Victoria. He later became George V.

In May 1927, the Federal Parliament House, Canberra, was opened by his son, also the Duke of York, who later became George VI. He was the father of the present Queen Elizabeth II.

By 1900 the women of South Australia and Western Australia were allowed to vote in colonial elections. Women in other colonies were not. New South Wales granted them the vote in 1902, Tasmania in 1903, Queensland in 1905 and Victoria in 1908. Voting in Commonwealth (Federal) elections was granted to all in

1902 except 'Asiatics, Africans and Australian Aborigines'.

When Federation was declared on January 1, 1901, the flag most commonly flown was the Union Jack of Great Britain. A competition for a new, Australian, flag design was held in that year and the winning flag flown for the first time on September 3, 1901. The 'winner' was a combination of five similar designs which underwent minor changes in later years but which was not widely accepted until 1914 and World War I.

Aborigines had virtually no voice at all in 1900 and were under the control of the different colonies. When Federation was declared, the Constitution stated that in counting the numbers of people in the Commonwealth, Aborigines would 'not be counted'. So the States, as they became known, kept power over the Aboriginal people. This meant that their treatment, including any rights, wages, conditions of work, health matters and other issues, varied considerably from state to state.

By December 31, 1900, Australia saw itself as leaving behind a history of separate colonies which had kept it divided since the start of white settlement and instead of facing a new century as one people with one destiny.

# VASHTI FARRER

Vashti Farrer was born in 1942. She has an MA in English Literature and loves theatre, acting, history, archaeology and quirky characters. Ghost writing for Kitty Barnes enabled her to indulge all these interests.

Vashti writes for all ages and has had over 60 adult short stories published as well as articles and book reviews. She has also written plays, poetry and stories for primary and secondary school and is a regular contributor to *School Magazine*.

*Plagues and Federation* is her fourth historically based novel for 9-14 year olds. Others include *Escape to Eaglehawk*, *Eureka Gold* and *Ned's Kang-u-roo*.

Vashti's great-uncle went to the Boer War, and she has always been interested in the Rocks area of Sydney and the movement towards Federation.

She is married with three adult children and a four-year-old granddaughter. She shares a house and garden with a dog, two cats, possums and blue-tongued lizards.